Estanislao – Warri

D0546984

Written by:
James David Adams, Jr., PhD, Associate Professor,
University of Southern California, Los Angeles, CA
90089.

Published by:
Abedus Press, PO Box 8018, La Crescenta, CA
91224

ISBN 0-9763091-2-2
First printing 2006

Library of Congress Control Number: 2006901427
Adams, James David
Estanislao – Warrior, Man of God – First Ed.
ISBN 0-9763091-2-2

Estanislao – Warrior, Man of God

God has blessings for everyone

Estanislao - Warrior, Man of God

Dedicated to Linda and Elliott

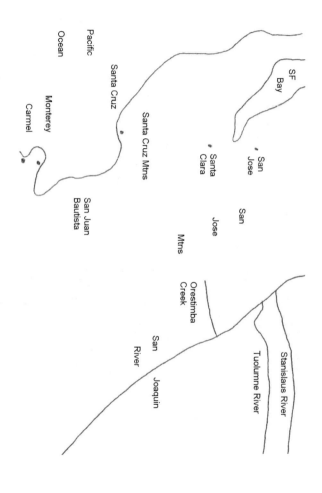

Estanislao 1. Winter is the time when people go hungry

Cucunuchi hiked deliberately as he ascended the canyon. His wife, daughter and mother were not far behind him. His wife and daughter were called Youatae (pronounced Yo-attay) and Lanucuye (pronounced Lannucuyay). His mother was Pitzenete (pronounced Peetzanatay). It was a cold and windy day. The fog was being blown from the bay over the hilltops and would soon cover them. They were all dressed in deer skin shirts and pants. His wife, daughter and mother wore elk skin moccasins. Cucunuchi (pronounced Cucunu-chee) was barefoot. The adults took turns carrying the 4 year old girl, who could not walk very far. Each adult carried a burden basket containing their belongings, especially their rabbit fur blankets. They had needed their blankets the previous night. It had been cold as they lay near the fire beside a large boulder. The burden baskets were made of willow and could carry heavy loads. There had been little to eat as they hiked. They found some wild cherries early in the morning near the lake. In the middle of the day, they had found some elderberries. Fortunately, they had brought some venison jerky with them. The jerky would not last long. The salmon would soon run in the rivers. The salmon would turn the rivers red with their red colored bodies as they swam to the spawning areas. Perhaps they would be allowed to return to fish for salmon.

They ascended out of the canyon and arrived at the top of the ridge. They could see the broad valley beneath them and could see to the fog covered bay. The fog was blowing quickly over them. The women were tired from walking up the steep slope. It was not a good time to rest as they were exposed to the wind and cold. Cucunuchi asked them to continue walking until they found some shelter from the wind. They began to descend quickly. All of a sudden, Cucunuchi's mother stopped and gasped. She pointed and asked "Is that the Mission San Jose?" Her eldest son, Cucunuchi said "Yes mother, that is the famous Mission San Jose you have heard so much about. Is it as big as you thought it would be?" His mother replied "It looks big enough to hold several hundred people." It was the largest building she had ever seen. Cucunuchi had seen the mission several times. This was the first time for his mother and wife. His mother wondered "Will your brother, Canocce, be there to meet us?"

Of course, they had all seen the Spanish soldiers who had come to visit their homeland on the Laquisimas River (pronounced Lahqueeseemas). The Spanish had visited on three different occasions over the past few years and had brought a Spiritual Leader they called Padre with them. The Spanish had astonished them with their horses, guns and metal swords. Clearly the power of the Spanish was great. The

Padre had tried to speak to them. But the people did not understand Spanish. The Padre did not bother to try to learn the Yokuts (pronounced Yokutes) language. The Spanish had tried to persuade some of the Yokuts people to go to the Mission San Jose with them. One Yokuts man had been the first to join them, two years ago. He had lost his arm in a battle with a grizzly bear a few months before. The man was now called Pedro by the Spanish and had been allowed to return to visit his homeland and try to persuade others to join him at the Mission. Every winter when people became hungry, more Yokuts people decided to join the Spanish. Pedro had promised that the Mission had plenty of food for them. He told them they would learn to speak Spanish and to live in the Spanish ways. It was a good life, he promised. Then came the last Spanish visit to Laquisimas, just last Spring. Cucunuchi's brother Canocce (pronounced Cannoke-say), only eleven years old, was taken to the Mission.

They descended down the canyon until they got to some boulders surrounded by coast live oak trees where they could rest. The women took out their wild tobacco and ate a little to keep their hunger under control. Cucunuchi climbed up on a boulder and found the mortar holes left there by the Ohlone (pronounced Olonay) people who lived in this area. The Ohlone people would not welcome them as they passed through this area. Cucunuchi could not see a village nearby. Perhaps they could walk carefully and not be seen by the

Ohlone. Cucunuchi carried his bow made of sinew backed holly and arrows made of carrizo cane and chamise, just in case.

The women conferred with each other and decided that it was late in the day and this would be a good place to spend the night. Pitzenete said "It is late. We should spend the night here and continue to the Mission in the morning." Cucunuchi preferred to continue to the Mission. He said "It is not safe here. We are in Ohlone territory. Besides, there is no water here." However, there was no recent sign of the Ohlone in this area. Perhaps it would be safe here. Cucunuchi's wife said "The Ohlone will see us carrying burden baskets and will know that we are traveling to the Mission. They will let us pass." They dropped their burden baskets carefully to the ground and began to search for food and water.

As they continued down the canyon, they found water and some tule. They pulled up the tule and ate the roots. There were acorns in the trees, but they were bitter. There was no time to dry them, grind them and leach the bitterness out of them. There were no animals to be seen in this canyon, except some birds in the trees. Apparently, the Ohlone had hunted too well in this area. They collected firewood as they returned to their burden baskets. Cucunuchi took out his fire drill and placed it in a hole in his hearth stick with some dry leaves underneath the hearth stick. He spun the fire drill back and forth between his hands and quickly had an ember glowing on the leaves. He blew gently on the ember until the leaves burned. He placed the burning ember under the tinder they had collected and quickly had a fire going. They kept the fire small to avoid being seen by the Ohlone. They wrapped themselves in their rabbit fur blankets and prepared for the cold night ahead. Lanucuye and her mother slept together for extra warmth.

They rose before the sun appeared and headed down the canyon in the direction of the Mission. As they walked the sun began to light the clouds above them. Cucunuchi was surprised to not see any sign of the Ohlone people. There was not even one village in this large canyon. Youatae worried out loud "I am so skinny. Look at your mother and daughter. We are all too skinny. Do you think the Mission will feed us enough to survive the winter?" Cucunuchi had heard her worry like this many times before. They were going to the Mission in part because there was not enough food for them in the village. Normally the women fatten themselves in the fall preparing for the winter, the time when people go hungry. However, this year there was not enough food for his wife, mother and daughter to fatten themselves for the winter. There had been a drought during the Spring that had caused a major loss of water fowl, fish and other animals. He tried to comfort his wife "I have been told that the Mission has a lot of food. No one goes hungry at the Mission." Then they heard a sound they had never hear before. It was a clanging sound almost like thunder, but not as frightening.

The sound came from the direction of the Mission. Cucunuchi's mother said "Maybe the Mission is being destroyed. Perhaps we have arrived too late." They continued walking until they emerged from the bottom of the canyon and could see the Mission still standing, just a few miles away.

They continued toward the Mission until they came to many tule huts. It was good to see the familiar site of the rounded homes of native people. Some of them were built in the Yokuts style from willow poles covered with tule thatch. Many of the huts were built in the Ohlone style, smaller and higher than the Yokuts style. Cucunuchi called out the familiar Yokuts greeting. There was no reply. They continued around the village, calling out the greeting. Finally, an old woman came out of a hut and greeted them in Yokuts. They did not recognize her. She told them she was from the Mokelumne. Her people lived far from the Laquisimas people. She told them she was sick today and was staying home. She told them everyone was already at the Mission.

Cucunuchi and his family walked tentatively toward the Mission. Eventually they heard people inside the buildings. As they approached, a group of men emerged and walked toward them. One of them said in Yokuts "Some newcomers have come out of the hills to join us." Another said "You should not have come today. The breakfast was not good." Another laughed and said "They will not be eating breakfast anyway." Pedro came out of the group and greeted them in the Yokuts way. He clasped arms, with his one good arm, with Cucunuchi and hugged the women. He said "Cucunuchi, it is good to see you and your family. Welcome to the Mission San Jose. You have walked a long way. Do you wish to rest? Or would you like to meet the Padre?" Cucunuchi was surprised at this greeting. It was traditional for Yokuts people to invite guests to eat. Cucunuchi said "Is my brother, Canocce here? We have not seen him for many months. Is he still alive?" Pedro said "He will be here later. He is already working in the fields." Cucunuchi said "We have come to join the Mission. We can start by meeting the Padre."

Pedro asked them to wait for him to return. He went into the building beside the Mission. The other people left Cucunuchi and his family to wait for the Padre. They were kept waiting in front of the Mission for a long time. They put down their burden baskets and sat on the ground. Their hunger was great. They ate a little wild tobacco to decrease their hunger. Cucunuchi's mother became worried that perhaps they were not welcome here. They were being shunned by the Padre and would have to return home.

Finally, a fat, bald man with very pale, white skin wearing a large brown robe emerged from the building. Pedro and a small woman were next to him. Cucunuchi's wife did not want to look at Padre Narciso Duran for fear that he was a creature from the underworld. Yokuts people were never that pale. The small woman approached them and offered them water. The Padre spoke to

them in Spanish, which they did not understand.
Fortunately, Pedro was there to translate into
Yokuts. He said, "The Padre invites you to drink.
You have walked a long way." The Padre spoke
again. Pedro translated, "What is your intention
in coming here?" Cucunuchi answered "We are
here to join the Mission San Jose and to learn the
Spanish ways." Pedro translated this for the Padre.
The Padre spoke again. Pedro said "Are you
willing to give up everything, learn the ways of God
and join the Holy Catholic Church?" Cucunuchi
said "Yes." Pedro asked each member of the family
the same question. Each said "Yes." The Padre
spoke again. This time he looked very serious and
concerned. Pedro said "You must not take this vow
lightly. If you join the Church, you will be giving
everything, even your life to the Church." Each
member of the family repeated their intention to
join the Church. Youatae instructed her daughter,
Lanucuye to say that she too would join the Church.

The Padre approached each member of
the family and thrust some leaves into their mouths.
Pedro instructed them that they were being purged
of the evil foods they had eaten before coming to
the Mission. They must chew and swallow the
leaves. From now on, they must not eat the native
plants or animals. These plants and animals were
evil, poison and must be avoided. Eating them
would only bring evil and death. Cucunuchi thought
this was very odd. His people had eaten the plants
and animals for countless years. Why are they now
evil? As he chewed the leaves he felt the familiar

burning sensation of tobacco. He asked Pedro "Is this some kind of tobacco we have been asked to eat?" Pedro said "Yes, it is a tobacco the Padre brought to the Mission from far away." Cucunuchi instructed his daughter to spit out the leaves. She was too young for tobacco and might die if she chewed so much tobacco.

Within a few minutes Cucunuchi began to feel very nauseous. His mother and wife started to vomit. Cucunuchi soon was vomiting also. There was nothing in their stomachs since they had not eaten since dinner the previous day. The vomiting was very painful. Cucunuchi found himself on his hands and knees in front of the Mission, retching in pain. After awhile, he began to see light around him. It was as if the Mission was glowing from its own light. He looked toward the door of the Mission and saw a pale man with white hair dressed in white. He appeared to be standing in front of the sun. Sun rays beamed from behind him. Cucunuchi recognized that he was having a sacred dream, hallucination induced by the tobacco. He had experienced a tobacco sacred dream, hallucination once before. But it was not this strong. He stayed on his knees looking at the image for many minutes until it passed.

Cucunuchi spoke to his family and Pedro. "I have had a dream. I saw a man in white with white hair standing in front of the sun. The light was almost blinding." His mother said "I have been in too much pain to see anything." Pedro knew the power of these dreams and said "This is a good sign. Cucunuchi has seen a powerful dream that tells us you are being welcomed with light." The Yokuts people used native plants to induce sacred dreams, religious hallucinations and tell the future. Cucunuchi's dream was a very good omen that they were doing the right thing. Their futures would be bright. Cucunuchi said "The Padre has been very good to us by giving me this dream. He is surely a powerful, spiritual man. I will learn his ways and the ways of his Church." Pedro translated this to the Padre who was confused. The Padre had never seen a tobacco induced hallucination before and had no idea that tobacco could induce sacred dreams. Finally, the Padre said "I am sure the dream means nothing. He is just seeing things because he is tired and full of the evil of the outside world." The Padre spoke briefly to Pedro and the woman, then walked away.

Pedro helped Cucunuchi to his feet. He said "Come. We must get you some new clothes so you will look like a Manso. All of us wear the same clothes." Manso is the Spanish word for tame Indian. The small woman escorted Cucunuchi's wife, daughter and mother into the building beside the Mission. Pedro lead Cucunuchi in the same door and took him into a small room. He instructed Cucunuchi to remove all his clothing and jewelry, including his hair decorations. Pedro left the room and came back in a few minutes with an armload of white clothes. He instructed Cucunuchi in how to dress in the woolen pants and shirt. He then took his Laquisimas clothes and instructed him to follow.

They went into a courtyard between the Mission and the adjoining buildings. Cucunuchi said "These new clothes are scratchy. My deerskin clothes are much more comfortable." Pedro made a pile of the clothes and burden baskets. Eventually the women emerged wearing white shirts and skirts. The small woman placed their clothes on the pile with the other clothes. Pedro went to a fire burning nearby and removed a burning stick. He used the stick to begin to burn the pile of clothes and burden baskets. Cucunuchi's mother complained "That is everything we own. Why are you burning our possessions?" Pedro answered "The Padre wants me to burn everything. This is what is done for all new arrivals." Black smoke rose up from the burning deer skin clothing. The smell of burning hides was powerful. Cucunuchi watched as his bow and arrows burned. He had worked many long weeks to make them. He had been very fond of the bow. Apparently, the Padre did not want him to hunt for the Mission.

Soon the loud, thunderous noise was heard again. Cucunuchi and his family cringed from the sound. Pedro said "That is the bell. Don't be afraid. The bell is calling all the Mansos to come for lunch." Pedro showed them where the bell hung in the tower above the mission. Cucunuchi asked "What is that huge bell made of?" Pedro said "The Padre tells me it is made of iron. Apparently, iron is something they find in Spain, where the Padre comes from." Cucunuchi had never heard any man made thing so loud. Even the large foot drums made by the Miwok people from sycamore logs, were not this loud.

Within a few minutes, many Mansos began to gather in the courtyard. The Padre emerged from the Mission carrying a large bowl with water in it. He called to the Mansos in Spanish. "Come and gather round. We have some new arrivals today. They come from over the hills, from Pedro's village. I will baptize them before we have lunch." Pedro brought Cucunuchi and his family to the Padre. Pedro instructed Cucunuchi to kneel. The Padre said "I Padre Buenaventura Fortuni, in the name of Jesus Christ, baptize you Estanislao (pronounced Aystanneeslou, ou as in ouch) in honor of the patron saint of Poland, on this Monday, September 24, 1821." He dipped his hand in the water and placed his hand on Cucunuchi's head. Then the Padre said "Rise my son and follow the teachings of the Church." Pedro instructed him to rise. His mother, wife and daughter were baptized next and given the names Orencia (pronounced Oraynceea), Estanislaa (pronounced Aystanneesla) and Sexta (pronounced Sayta). The Padre went back into the Mission to write in his baptismal record that he had baptized the 28 year old Estanislao, the 22 year old Estanislaa, the 50 year old Orencia and the 4 year old Sexta. It was a good day for the Mission.

Estanislao was surprised by the baptism. He felt nothing and did not find it an especially meaningful ceremony. This was the ceremony that made him a Catholic. Yet it was a very simple ceremony. Perhaps the Spanish found meaning

in simplicity. The Padre was elegantly robed, but
no one else was dressed up for the occasion. The
Padre had chanted one song, but there had been
no clapper sticks, flutes, whistles, dancing or group
singing. Estanislao was used to the elaborate
Yokuts ceremonies where the whole village
dressed in their regalia and sang and danced. For
Estanislao, the important ceremony had been the
tobacco induced sacred dream, hallucination.

From out of the crowd of Mansos came
Canocce. He was only 12 years old. He embraced
his mother warmly, but did not speak to her. His
mother spoke to him, told him how much she
had missed him and how good it was to see him
again. She had so much to tell him. Yet she was
surprised that he did not speak. Pedro spoke for
him. He said "Your son, has been baptized Orencio
(pronounced Oraynceeo). You must call him by
his Spanish name. He is not allowed to speak to
you in the Yokuts language. He must speak to you
in Spanish. I alone am allowed to speak to you in
Yokuts during this first month. This is to help you
learn Spanish." The poor woman began to cry.
"My own son cannot speak to me?" Pedro calmed
her. "He can speak to you in Spanish." Orencia
was frustrated. "But I will not understand him. I
have not seen him for several months. Surely, he
can say something to me."

Orencio began to cry also. He spoke to
her in Spanish. "Mother, it is good to see you,
my brother and sister-in-law. I have missed
you." Pedro translated this into Yokuts for him.

He continued. "I have learned much here in the Mission. I work hard every day and can speak Spanish well." At this point a woman called everyone in to lunch. Orencio said "We will talk again. Now is the time to eat. Come with me and have some lunch."

They went into the side building beside the Mission and continued down the hall to the kitchen. In the kitchen, they were each given a bowl, spoon and cup. The bowl contained beans and meat. The cup contained water. Each received a tortilla. Estanislao had never seen food like this before. He was used to food cooked over an open fire or cooked in the coals under the fire. He had never seen rice or beans before. He had no idea what a spoon was or how to use it. He dutifully carried his lunch as his brother did. They all went to a table and sat at a bench. Orencio showed them how to use the spoon and eat from the bowl. The spoon was not hard to use but was less efficient than eating with the fingers. Estanislao copied some of the men and used the tortilla to scoop up the food and eat with his fingers. The cup was just like drinking from a Yokuts basket. Orencia and Estanislaa were both very skilled at making water tight baskets lined with asphaltum to drink from. The bowls were similar to the Yokuts basket trays that were used to serve food at home. The food tasted good, especially since they were very hungry. Even the girl, Sexta did not complain about the food. Estanislao still felt uncomfortable and somewhat nauseous from the tobacco the Padre had administered. He ate slowly and carefully. Orencia and Estanislaa went back to ask for more food. They were given a little more to eat.

After lunch was siesta time. This consisted of a two hour nap. Most of the men simply sat down against a wall somewhere and dozed. Estanislao sat near Orencio. The women and girl were taken inside to lie down and rest. After the siesta, everyone went back to their work, including Orencio, who was busy digging an irrigation ditch. Estanislao had no idea why anyone would want to dig a ditch to allow water to flow. He had seen beavers dig ditches to direct the flow of water for their own uses. He did not know why men would do this. His wife and daughter came out of the building and told him they had been told to lie on beds made of straw and horse hair. They had never seen beds before and were used to lying on the floor. Estanislao had heard that the Chumash lie on raised platforms above the ground, similar to the Spanish beds.

Pedro came to Estanislao and instructed him to help dig the irrigation ditch. He ran to catch up to Orencio. They walked in silence to the ditch, about two miles away. Estanislao was amazed to see that the ditch was very long. He could not see the end of it. He asked Orencio how long he had been working on the ditch. Orencio did not answer. Several other Mansos were there already digging with large digging sticks and the shoulder blades of large animals. Estanislao had never seen such huge shoulder blades before. He picked up a shoulder blade and began to dig following his younger brother's example. He asked what animal the bone came from. His brother answered him in Spanish, "an ox."

Estanislao asked many questions about the ditch and why they were digging. None of the Mansos could answer him in Yokuts, only Pedro was allowed to do this. But Pedro was not there. They tried to speak to him in Spanish. Estanislao had no idea what they were saying. They tried to teach him some words of Spanish as they worked. They taught him how to say stick, dig, ditch, shoulder blade and ox in Spanish.

They worked for almost three hours when they heard the Mission bell. Everyone dropped their tools and started to walk back to the Mission. Estanislao preferred to run. He called to Orencio to run with him. He ran slowly so his younger brother could keep up. They had run together many times, especially with their father. As they ran, Estanislao noticed that there were large fields of plants he had never seen before. He did not know what the plants were. He asked Orencio to identify the plants for him. Orencio told him the Spanish names for the plants, wheat, beans, corn, oats, squash, grapes, figs, olives and others.

When they returned to the Mission, they met Orencia, Estanislaa and Sexta. They ate dinner together. Estanislao was impressed with how earnestly the Padre prayed before they ate. Pedro told him that the Padre blessed their food and blessed them when he prayed. Estanislao thought this was good.

After dinner, Estanislao, the women and the girl were taken to a room where they would learn Spanish. Orencio and many others went to another room to learn about the Catholic faith. The Spanish instructor was a fat, bald Padre. They were instructed to call him Padre Jose. There were twenty other students who were learning the basics of Spanish with them. The Padre was a patient teacher and even laughed from time to time. But if they spoke Yokuts, he swatted them with a long, slender stick. Padre Jose could not speak Yokuts or Ohlone, but could recognize when these languages were being spoken. He was very strict about insisting that they spoke only Spanish.

After studying Spanish for nearly two hours, they were exhausted. The women had worked all afternoon scrubbing walls and floors in the buildings. They did not understand why the Spanish liked to keep the rooms so clean. It was unnatural to have no dirt or dust in a room. All Yokuts houses and buildings had dirt floors. Estanislao was told to go to a room and sleep with the bachelors. The women and girl were taken to another room to sleep. Their room was locked at night. Estanislao did not like sleeping on the Spanish bed. The floor was more comfortable.

In the morning, Estanislao found Pedro and asked him why he was not allowed to sleep with his family. Pedro answered "You are not married according to the Catholic Church. You must not sleep with your wife until you are married in the

Church." Estanislao said "I married her several years ago. I paid several chok for her. Her father gave us permission to marry." A chok (pronounced choke) was a length of beads on a string that circled around the hand. The chok was a unit of Yokuts' money. Pedro said "I understand that you have been married according to the Yokuts tradition. You must now be married according to the Catholic tradition. You can only be married after you have learned enough Spanish and enough of the catechism to recite the vows." This was irritating to Estanislao. He had been baptized. He wore the Manso clothes. He worked on the ditch. Yet he could not sleep with his own wife. Pedro laughed. "This is how they get you to learn Spanish."

Estanislao worked all day on the irrigation ditch, which he learned would bring water from the nearby canyon for the wheat and other fields. He learned that the Spanish had brought all these plants with them from Spain. He saw several Mansos out in the fields tending the crops. He learned that the crops had to be weeded, watered and kept free of bugs. This was a very important job, especially since many of the crops would be ready to harvest soon. That evening he studied Spanish diligently and was not swatted once by Padre Jose.

His life continued this way until Sunday which was the day of worship. Everyone gathered in the Mission Chapel early in the morning. All the Mansos stood in the Chapel. Padre Fortuni lead

the mass. Estanislao did not understand what
was happening during the service. He did his best
to mumble when everyone else responded to the
Padre. He knelt when they knelt and tried to follow
along. He was impressed with the ceremony. He
had never heard singing like he heard in the mass.
The melodies were unlike any Yokuts melodies. He
was moved as he heard the songs echo against
the massive Mission walls. A musical instrument
played music that was completely captivating. It
was loud and resounded like thunder. A man sat
on a bench and touched the instrument to make
it play. Orencio told him the instrument was an
organ. Estanislao held his breath to make sure he
heard every note. He found himself having to force
himself to breathe. The music was enthralling. He
was disappointed when the music ended and the
Padre spoke. He wanted to hear more music. The
service lasted more than two hours.

After the service, Estanislao stood in the
church with the sounds of the music still ringing
in his head. He did not want to move. This was
fantastic, better than he had imagined. He saw
some of the Mansas go toward the altar and kneel
to pray. Then he saw a carved statue high on the
altar. He recognized the figure immediately. It was
a man with the rays of the sun streaming around
him. He had never seen artwork that so carefully
resembled a person before. All Yokuts art was
more abstract, less clearly defined. He found the
art to be too much a copy. Surely the man in the
statue was upset to have his image so clearly

copied. He asked Orencio, "Who is the man in the statue?" Orencio said, "That is God." Estanislao said "I saw God in my tobacco dream." Orencio advised him in a low voice speaking Yokuts "Don't tell others about your dream. The Padre would not like it." Estanislao found this very confusing. He had seen God in a sacred dream induced by the Padre. Surely this was good. Estanislao spent the rest of the day learning Spanish from the other Mansos, at least until his questions annoyed them.

He was able to see Estanislaa briefly. She said that she was happy and learning much about cooking Spanish food. She already knew how to cook beans in a big pot. She told Estanislao that the pot was made of iron. When the pot was placed directly over the fire, the flames did not damage the pot. The Yokuts cooked with water tight baskets by placing hot stones in them and stirring with a stick to prevent the basket from burning. Estanislaa thought that baskets were better to cook with, because they could be made at the Mission by the Mansas. The pots had to come from Spain. Estanislaa complained that Sunday was not a day of rest. She worked just as hard cooking on Sunday as she did every other day.

That evening he heard the loud clatter of many horses approaching the Mission. He saw thirty five Spanish soldiers riding toward the Mission. The Mansos began to move away from where the soldiers would come. Orencio advised Estanislao "Stay away from the soldiers. They are always looking for an excuse to hurt someone."

Estanislao had seen this already. When the soldiers came with a Padre to the Laquisimas village, they had dragged away a Yokuts who was visiting the village. Estanislao had learned that the Yokuts was actually a Manso who had left the Mission to visit his family, but had not returned to the Mission. The soldiers had whipped the Manso and took him away in shackles.

The soldiers lived in the Presidio near the Mission. Estanislao learned that the soldiers' job was to protect the Mission and to help recruit new Mansos. He had not seen them before in their fancy dress uniforms they wore as they approached the Mission, with their brass buttons and polished swords glinting in the evening sun. The soldiers he had seen in the village all wore heavy leather jackets and large metal helmets. Orencio said "The soldiers are returning from the Mission Carmel. They have been gone for over two weeks." Two Padres came out of the Mission to watch the soldiers approach. They waved to the soldiers. The Padres seemed happy to see the soldiers come back.

Estanislao was very interested in the horses. The soldier's horses were grand animals with huge muscular legs. They were much grander animals than any animal found in Yokuts territory, except for the grizzly bear. He wanted to learn how to ride a horse and to ride like the wind. The power of the horses was overwhelming. Then he saw an object being pulled by a horse. Orencio called it a cart. The cart had round objects that made it travel easily as the horse pulled it. Orencio said the round objects were wheels. Estanislao had never seen wheels before. Surely the Spanish were of great intelligence to be able to invent wheels. The cart held many guns and some ammunition.

Guns were familiar to Estanislao. He had seen the Spanish soldiers shoot their guns at targets made of wood in his village. The sound was even louder than the Mission bell. It was as if thunder had been put into a stick. The thunder could be made to sound when a man pulled a trigger. The thunder made a bullet come out of the gun and travel faster than the eye could see. Guns were very powerful weapons, more powerful than bows and arrows. Arrows could be stopped by shields of thick leather. Estanislao had been told the Spanish wore thick leather vests to stop Yokuts arrows. Bullets could go through almost anything. Thick wood and rocks could stop bullets.

The next day, Estanislao and Orencio ran to the ditch to continue their work. As they ran, a soldier came up behind them on his horse. He rode beside them and watched them run. He laughed and said "A Spaniard rides. Mansos run." He rode off, leaving dust behind him. Estanislao watched him ride off. He and Orencio continued running. Estanislao noticed that after a short time, the Soldier stopped his horse, turned the horse around and allowed the horse to walk back toward them. This was interesting to Estanislao. As they ran by the Soldier, he thought that the horse had not run long.

After working on the ditch for awhile, Estanislao developed large arm and shoulder muscles. He had not needed such arm and shoulder muscles before. He was happy working on the ditch. It was good to work hard. The Yokuts believed that hard work was good for health. His health had been good since coming to the Mission, except that he missed Estanislaa and Sexta.

After siesta, Estanislao and Orencio began to run back to the ditch. Several soldiers rode up behind them. One of the said, "These Mansos run well. Do you think they can run faster than a horse?" Another said, "I bet 1 peso that the big Manso can run faster than Juan's horse from here to that oak tree and back." The bet was made. Estanislao would race a horse to a distant oak tree and back, about 2 miles. The horse was powerful and impatient. Estanislao was instructed to start first. He started running as fast as he could. After awhile, he heard the horse thundering behind him. Soon the soldier and horse flew past him. Estanislao continued to run. By the time he got to the oak tree, he saw that the horse was slowing down. When he was about half way back from the oak tree, he caught up to the horse. He saw that the horse was sweating intensely, which made a white froth in its hair. Saliva flowed from its mouth. The horse was breathing very heavily and tried to keep up with him as he ran by. Soon, the horse could not run any more, and started to walk. No matter how much the soldier whipped his horse, the horse could run no more. As Estanislao ended the race, the other soldiers laughed loudly and slapped each other on the back. They were delighted to see Juan lose the race. They had known that a fast human runner can outrun a horse on a long course. Juan, of course, was incensed, and said to Estanislao "You think you are clever to outrun my horse. There will be a time when your cleverness will not be enough." Estanislao sensed that he had made an enemy.

The harvest time arrived quickly, since it was a cold Fall. Estanislao learned how to harvest wheat, corn and beans. The work was easy, but had to be done carefully to avoid spoiling the crops. Estanislao had never worked so much with plants before. This was considered women's work by the Yokuts. Although men did help. The amount of food harvested was huge in Estanislao's opinion. The men carefully harvested the wheat with large scythes. The wheat was then taken into the court yard to be threshed by the women and older children. The beans had to be dried before they could be stored. This was done by placing them in large wooden boxes in the court yard. The boxes had to be watched constantly to keep the birds and squirrels away. The corn was hung from the rafters of storage rooms and left there to dry. The corn was simply stored hanging. The wheat and beans were stored in large wooden boxes inside large rooms. Estanislao was astonished how quickly the harvest was completed. Everyone in the Mission worked on the harvest. It was a happy time, with everyone working together. At the end of the harvest, Padre Fortuni said a special harvest celebration Mass. He dressed in special, expensive robes recently imported from Spain.

Estanislao had seen corn before. The Cahuilla and Mojave people grew corn that was similar to the Spanish corn. The Padre told Estanislao that corn came from New Spain, not from Old Spain. The Spanish had learned to plant corn from Indians in the south called Aztecs. Estanislao was amazed that the Spanish would want to plant corn. The Yokuts people thought corn was not fit to eat. The Cahuilla and Mojave had to plant it and eat it because they were so unfortunate as to live in the desert, where few plants grew. The Yokuts lived on more bountiful land where they could survive on what God gave them and did not need corn.

Estanislao noticed that some of the children had no thumbs on their right hands or lacked the final joint of their thumbs. These children could not do much of the harvest work, since a thumb is so important for picking up the harvested plants. They tended to drop as much of a load as they picked up. He asked Orencio why the children had no thumbs. Orencio took Estanislao a little way away from Spanish ears and told him in a low voice. "Do you remember last Spring when the Spanish came to Laquisimas? You were out hunting geese with many of the men. The Spanish drove away or killed many of the women. I saw the soldiers rape some of the women before they were killed. Their leader was called Sanchez. Then they rounded up the children and selected the children who were about seven to fifteen years old. The others they drove away or killed. The children they wanted were placed in a line. Our thumbs were tied to a long rope they call riata. We were lead all the way to the Mission with our thumbs tied to the rope. I was very careful to loosen the rope a little so it did not turn my thumb blue. But, some of the children were not so careful. Many of them lost their thumbs or part of their thumbs." Estanislao was shocked to hear this. On the one hand, he had to admit the Spanish were clever to take the children who were old enough to take care of themselves, but not strong enough to rebel. But he was shocked the Spanish had been so stupid as to tie the children so they would lose their thumbs and not be good workers.

Estanislao said to Orencio "We must tell the Padre of these sins. Surely the soldiers who committed these sins will be punished. The Padres have taught me that killing, raping and kidnapping are sins." Orencio quickly hushed him. "Don't ever mention what happened in Laquisimas to anyone. What the Spanish do is not considered a sin." Orencio then told Estanislao to depart so they would not arouse any suspicion.

Work on the ditch, called a zanja, continued slowly. There were many stones to move. The ground had to be carefully graded to make the water flow slowly down hill. Several of the Mansos had already learned how to grade the ditch properly. It was slow, careful work. But

Estanislao's work on Spanish proceeded quickly. After two months, Padre Jose decided that Estanislao and Estanislaa knew enough Spanish that they could be married in the eyes of the Holy Catholic Church.

Padre Jose conducted the ceremony during the siesta time. A few Mansos attended as well as Orencio, Orencia and Sexta. They all laughed that a husband and wife should have to be married again. Padre Jose instructed them that their Yokuts marriage meant nothing to the Catholic Church. Now that they were married in the Catholic Church, this meant they were married before God. Estanislao wondered why the Spanish did not believe the Yokuts marriage meant anything to God. The Padre explained to him that the Yokuts people lived under the care of God, but could never go to heaven, since they were not baptized in the Church. This troubled Estanislao, since his father had never been baptized. Still it was good to finally be able to sleep with his wife again. He was allowed to construct a Yokuts tule hut for his family to live in. Orencio would have to live with the bachelors. But his wife, daughter and mother could live in the tule hut. Estanislao and Orencio spent many hours building the hut during the siesta time. Some of the Mansos helped. They were careful to build it in the traditional Yokuts way with as much attention to detail as if they were making a basket.

When the tule hut was finished, Estanislao and Estanislaa were very happy. They could finally live together as a family again. They held a brief celebration after dinner and invited all the Mansos to come and see their new home. Pedro came by and said a prayer to bless the new house. Inside the house was very plain with a dirt floor, a fire pit and a few of their belongings hanging from the willow poles that supported the tule mats. This was very similar to the home they had in Laquisimas.

Estanislaa was very happy. She was allowed to sleep with her husband again. She had a house again. But her real happiness came from the fact that she was now fat enough to survive the winter. She, her daughter and mother-in-law had eaten well every day until they put on the fat they needed to survive the winter. She told Estanislao how happy she was that now she could survive the winter. Estanislao had noticed that all of the women in the mission were fat. This was the custom for preparation for the winter, so he was happy too. But he kept thinking about all the food that had been harvested. He could not help thinking that the women did not have to be that fat to survive the winter, when so much food was stored away.

It was now winter, the time when people go hungry. Estanislao saw that the Mission still had food during the winter. The Spanish knew how to store food during the winter. The Yokuts stored acorns, dried fish, dried deer meat, and medicines during the winter. But some years, the stored foods did not last the entire winter. This meant that the hunters had to go out into the cold to find food for the people. The Spanish had cattle and horses that were slaughtered as needed to feed the Mansos. The Spanish life was much easier than the Yokuts life, at least in terms of food.

Estanislao was very careful and respectful to the Spanish, especially the soldiers. He had learned very quickly that even the slightest disrespect resulted in whipping. He had seen several Mansos suffer from whipping. Their shirts were removed. They were put against a wall, or asked to lie down. Then the whip was applied, usually about 25 times. Sometimes, even the Mansas, women, were whipped. Even one boy had been whipped. The whipping had been so severe that he died. The Padre who had administered the whipping had to do penance to make up for killing the boy. The Padre had repented, but had said that at least he knew the boy went to heaven, instead of dying a heathen's death.

After the harvest, the soldiers used the fields for their military drills. Estanislao watched the drills with interest. At first, he thought the drills were a waste of time. The Sargeant seemed very eager to show his men that he was boss. The men had to follow his orders quickly or suffer the consequences. Estanislao wondered if the purpose of the drills was mostly to establish the order of who was boss and who should follow orders. But as the days passed, Estanislao came to realize that the drills were actually preparation for war. The men were being taught how to go to battle in a simple, step by step process. They started out marching in ranks. The Mansos watched the marching and were amazed that the soldiers would march in step. This was completely unlike anything the Yokuts would ever do. Among the Yokuts, each man followed his own path, in his own way, provided that everyone ended up working for the common good. Estanislao watched and eventually thought that marching in formation would be a very good way to break through a line of men during battle. Estanislao made sure that he took time every day to watch as much of the drills as he could. He was very keen on watching the drills that involved horses. The soldiers had several drills that involved charging the enemy while on horseback. These tactics would be extremely effective against an enemy on foot.

He learned much about the Spanish guns. They could shoot a bullet a long distance, longer than arrows could fly. They were about as accurate as an arrow. But they were very slow to reload. An arrow could be reloaded on the bow much faster. But bullets could penetrate much better than any arrow. The bullets could penetrate through almost anything, except stone and thick wood. The soldiers had target practice almost every week. They had to be careful not to use too many bullets, since lead, flints and gun powder had to be brought all the way from Spain. The Spanish also had cannons that were not fired often. Although they were always dragged around during the battle drills. The cannons could fire a large, lead ball for a very long distance. The ball was heavier than any stone of similar size. The ball made a large hole in the ground when it hit. Clearly cannon balls could penetrate much more than a bullet. Firing a cannon required a large amount of gun powder.

In December, the Padre in Spanish class started to prepare them for Christmas. Estanislao knew that this was the celebration of Jesus' birth. Jesus was God who had come to earth to help men learn the proper way to live and to worship God. Estanislao was amazed that God would come to earth. The Yokuts God was unapproachable, or if approached, death would surely follow. Only certain elite people were allowed to learn about the Yokuts God. Jesus was so approachable, personal. Estanislao learned as much as he could about Jesus and Christmas. When Christmas finally came, the Mission was decorated with California Holly branches with dark green leaves and groups of bright red berries. There were many more candles than usual. Padre Fortuni dressed in his frock that had just come from Spain. The frock was grand with gold thread on white cloth. The Padre wore a large head dress in the same colors. All the Mansos were impressed with the new clothes. Estanislao felt left out. In the village, all the people would dress in their regalia for such a sacred festival. The feathered regalia was only worn for special, social gatherings and sacred times. The Mansos only wore their normal work clothes. The message of the mass was that God has blessings for all of us. The mass was special with the singing of Christmas music. All the Mansos sang fervently. Estanislao was moved by the music and found himself dancing as he would in the village. Padre Jose was standing in the back of the Mission and saw Estanislao dancing. A Manso quickly told Estanislao not to dance. Estanislao remembered that dancing was not allowed in the Mission. In the Yokuts village dancing was a sacred way to pray. Each dance was a prayer.

Estanislao stopped dancing. But it was too late. The Padre caught Estanislao by the back of the shirt. He dragged Estanislao out into the court yard. Estanislao was surprised that the fat Padre was so strong. It was as if he were impassioned with his rage. The Padre immediately started whipping Estanislao with a whip hanging on a nearby post. Estanislao felt five lashes hit him in the face and arms as he pleaded with the Padre that he was sorry for dancing. Blood flowed freely from his face in several places. He was on his knees and fell with his face down. The Padre continued to whip him ten more times on the back. Estanislao had been given a light punishment. He was left in the court yard. He could not move. The pain was tremendous. All he could think was, "God has blessings for all of us. How is this my blessing?" He lay there for many minutes until he could finally move. He carefully rose and walked slowly to his hut. After the mass, Estanislaa came to him and helped tend his wounds. She washed his wounds with soap and water. Estanislao slept until his wife brought him some dinner. It was hard to believe that he had been whipped brutally for dancing a prayer to Jesus.

Estanislaa continued to wash and treat his wounds. Estanislao healed quickly, but was not able to return to work for three days. On the fourth day, a soldier came to their house and told Estanislao to get back to work or face another whipping. That day after work, he found Estanislaa in the house alone. He asked if she was all right. She did not respond. Estanislao could tell there was something very wrong. He went to his wife and comforted her. Eventually she told him what had happened. Padre Jose had come up behind her while she was making bread and tried to rape her. She had beaten him off with her rolling pin. He had scolded her for hitting him and told her she would be punished. At this, Estanislao was infuriated. He got up and went straight to Padre Buenaventura Fortuni. He felt that Fortuni might listen to him better than Padre Duran. Duran was more interested in keeping everything quiet in the Mission and not letting the outside world think there was trouble at the Mission. Fortuni was more open to listening to personal problems. Estanislao marched into Padre Fortuni's office, a small, dark room full of papers and books. Fortuni looked up and said, "Estanislao, what is it my son?" Estanislao told him, "Padre Jose tried to rape my wife." Padre Fortuni did not seem upset by this news. He appeared somewhat displeased with Estanislao as he said, "Padre Jose would never try to rape anyone. He has taken vows of chastity. Estanislao, be very careful before you charge him with such a terrible crime." Estanislao said, "Padre. He came up behind my wife while she was making bread, pulled up her skirt and tried to insert himself into her." The Padre looked confused, as if Estanislao had not spoken Spanish correctly. He asked Estanislao to repeat himself. After more questioning the Padre said, "Well, clearly no crime has been committed. You and she, both admit he did not rape her. I believe there is a much more reasonable explanation. Perhaps he was only trying to help clean her dress." Estanislao at this point was getting exasperated. He could not understand why the Padre, who was so quick to punish an Indian, was reluctant to believe that another Padre would do anything wrong. Estanislao said, "As you have told me many times, God is the one who judges us. I will leave the matter in his hands." The Padre said, "Very wisely said Estanislao. I will speak to Padre Jose about this matter." Estanislao left, still very angry and thinking "God has blessings for all of us. How is this a blessing?"

After dinner, Padre Fortuni called Padre Jose Viader to his office. He said to the Padre, "Jose, I hear that you pulled up the skirt of Estanislaa today." Padre Jose said, "Padre, I was only attempting to clean away some flour that she had clumsily spilled on her dress." Fortuni said, "I understand you became much more personal than that with her. I even hear you tried to rape her." Jose said, "You know how these Indians lie. How can you believe anything she would say about me?" Fortuni said, "This comes from someone else.

Someone I trust and believe, not from Estanislaa."
Jose said, "Padre, these Indians are only animals.
They are only one third human. There is no sin
of rape against animals." Fortuni said, "It is true
that the Indians are only one third human. But that
one third is very important to the Church and to
Spain. It is hoped they will become more human
in the future and be able to be good citizens of
Spain and good members of the Church. Besides,
I do not think you should be having relations with
animals either." Jose said, "Padre, have mercy.
She is such a new arrival, she is mostly savage
and untamed anyway." Fortuni said, "It is true that
she is still quite savage. But she has learned to
make good bread. She may become a fine citizen
one day. I do not think that God would want you
to be punished for rape. Perhaps you should do
penance for disheveling her skirt. Come to me
for confession next Thursday. I will give you one
hundred hail Mary's and take away your salary
for one week." Padre Jose was surprised. "You
punish me too severely for such a minor offense."
Fortuni said, "Yes, but this is not the first time you
have done this. I remember at least two other
Mansas with similar complaints about you in the
past." Padre Jose was quieted by these comments.
He said, "Yes Padre. I will be at confession this
week."

Estanislao had not seen sickness in the
Mission. In the Laquisimas village, sickness was
not uncommon. Fevers, colds, and pneumonia
were prevalent during the winter, especially.

Children were commonly victims of pneumonia. Death during childhood from pneumonia was more frequent than any parent wanted. As the cold rain started to pound the Mission, sickness came to the Mission. Several children died from pneumonia and the flu. The flu was a European introduction to California. The Indians had little resistance against the flu. Estanislao was surprised that the Spanish could do nothing for pneumonia. They simply waited and prayed. When the first child died, a brief funeral was held with more prayers that could not comfort the parents of the lost child. The Padres were frequently heard to say, "It is the will of God." The Yokuts people had several medicines that were used against pneumonia, with some success. Yerba Santa was especially sought for use in pneumonia. Many Yokuts people stored the dried leaves of Yerba Santa to use during the winter. The Yokuts people had personal prayers that were used when the plant was gathered and when the plant was administered to the child. The Yokuts believed that God had to be involved in the healing process. The parents of one child had begged the Padre to let them use Yerba Santa to treat their child. The Padre had forbidden it saying that the plant was either evil or not to be trusted. This puzzled Estanislao. Why did the Padre refuse to use a plant that his own followers knew was of use? The plant was a gift from God. An old woman told Estanislao that the Padres would never use anything they did not understand. The Padres assumed everything new to them was either evil or not to be trusted.

As Spring approached, the Mansos returned to the fields to plant their crops. Estanislao helped with the planting. He learned how to cut the weeds in the fields and plow the fields. Plowing was very difficult work that only the strongest men could perform. It involved hooking the plow to an ox and holding onto the wooden handles of the plow while the ox pulled the plow. The man had to push down on the handles to make the plow blade cut the soil to the right depth. It was exhausting work, that no man could do for more than about 3 hours a day. Then Estanislao learned how to walk through the fields scattering the seeds that would grow their crops for the next harvest.

Estanislaa and the women of the mission were still as fat as they had been before winter. She was very happy and had not suffered from hunger at all during the winter. In Laquisimas, she would have lost probably 30 pounds or more during the winter, all the time suffering from hunger. In the mission, she kept her weight all winter long. Estanislao noticed that this was true of all the women and the children. Some of the men were fat too. Estanislao kept himself thin and strong. This was the way God intended for him to be. This was the way God intended for men to be.

The ditch was almost complete and would soon bring water to the newly planted fields. The ditch was actually a supplement for the old ditch that did not bring in enough water for the expanded fields. During the winter, working on the ditch was easier, since the rain softened the dirt. However, they did not work during the rain, because the Padre feared that the Mansos might become sick.

Estanislao 2. Estanislao becomes Alcalde

Finally the irrigation ditch was complete. The ditch was several miles long and brought water from the stream to the fields near the Mission. The ditch was about two feet wide and carried quite a bit of water. The flow was as fast as any stream. This prevented plants from growing in the water and clogging the ditch. Estanislao and Orencio had a feeling of accomplishment. They had helped complete something that would benefit the entire Mission for many years to come. This was unlike tasks done for the Yokuts people, that were always of short term benefit, such as gathering acorns for the winter. The Yokuts did not build Missions and irrigation canals that were meant to last many years. The only task the Yokuts did as a people, with long term consequences, was war.

Estanislao remembered when he was a teenager. His father had come to him and told him it was time for him to die. It was time for the boy to die, and the man to be born. His mother had said "I will never see my boy again." This was his time to pass through the ordeal that would be the first step toward becoming a man. He had been asked to fast, pray and complete several tasks in silence for the village. He had helped cut brush that blocked the trail to the duck pond. He had helped construct racks to dry salmon. He had learned how to make the Yokuts top knot headdress and feathered dance skirt. After seven days of this ordeal, he had been taken by the Shaman of his village to the sweat lodge. There he was taught the prayer song of Datura wrightii, tahni (pronounced tahnee) in Yokuts, the plant that would help him talk to God and learn his future. He had stayed in the lodge all night and all day the next day, fasting, praying and being instructed in the ways of the Yokuts people by the Shaman. The next evening, he was ready to undergo the tahni uish (pronounced u-eesh) or Datura ceremony and had been given a preparation of tahni. The Shaman told him that he must be brave. Tahni was a challenge that not all boys survived. The Shaman told him that the amount of tahni that caused a vision was almost the same amount that stopped the breath. His mouth had become very dry. His vision became completely blurred. His skin felt hot and dry. The Shaman sang the tahni song over and over again, until Estanislao started to hear strange sounds. Then he started to see things he had never seen before. He had been told that an animal would guide him through his dream. After many confusing visions that he did not understand, a golden eagle flew into his vision and said "Follow." He followed the eagle who lead him to the river. At the river, the eagle told him to build a house of wood and protect his people. Then he vanished. Estanislao emerged from his vision. It was two days later. The Shaman told him he had stopped breathing several times. The Shaman had feared that he would die. But something had kept him alive. Estanislao told the Shaman of his vision. The Shaman then told him "From now on, you will not talk about your vision, because this would decrease the power of the medicine God has given you in this vision. The golden eagle will now be your power, your medicine and your spiritual guide."

After the tahni uish, Estanislao had been instructed in the ways of manhood, becoming brave. He was taught to make obsidian arrowheads, arrow shafts from carrizo, and sinew backed bows from juniper. He spent most of his time with the men, listening to their stories of hunting and warring. He learned that it was considered braver to touch an enemy with a hand or a war club than to kill an enemy. It was preferable to take an enemy as a slave than to kill him. When he was nearly fifteen, and had passed puberty, he was taken on his first deer hunt. He and several men spent the night fasting and praying in the sweat lodge. Before the sun came up, they washed themselves in the river to wash off the human smells and covered their bodies with deer skins. They went out to hunt dressed as deer. His job was to provide meat for the elderly in the village. On his first hunt, he had killed a small buck. He butchered the meat and gave it all to the eldest man in the village, who then divided it with others. Estanislao was not allowed to eat any of the meat from the buck he killed. If he had eaten the meat, he would have had bad luck hunting after that.

The wheat came up soon after planting

and grew quickly. The beans also grew quickly
and had to be tended carefully to prevent the vines
from strangling each other. In the meantime, the
cows were in need of tending. They had to be
kept away from the growing crops. Estanislao was
appointed to help care for the cows. The Padre
had ordered more cows from Spain. A ship was
due within the next month to bring the cows. The
cows were stupid and slow. Their meat tasted
good, but not as good as horse meat. The Mansos
watched the cows every day. They had to be
lead to fresh pastures and kept away from the
irrigation ditches. They had to be inspected for skin
diseases, breathing problems, hoof infections, eye
irritations and many other problems. Cows were
similar in many ways to the native California elk,
called tule (pronounced tulee) elk. They tended to
stay in small groups and follow each other single
file. But cows were slower and not as clever. One
of the soldiers told the Mansos that the cows were
bred in Spain to be slow and stupid, like a Manso.
Estanislao was amazed to hear that someone
would breed an animal for human purposes. Surely
this was contrary to what God wanted. God had
made the cows. Changing them through breeding
would upset the balance of nature that God had
created. When Estanislao discussed this with the
other Mansos, Pedro reminded him that the Yokuts
kept dogs for hunting. The Chihuahua and other
southern people bred small dogs to use as pets and
food. That evening at Spanish class, Estanislao
asked the Padre about how God felt about having

his cows changed to suit human purposes. The Padre reminded Estanislao of the Bible passage that God had created plants and animals for human use. Estanislao thought that surely God, who is perfect, knew how to best create cows for human use. Why did men think they could breed cows to make them better than God? Estanislao kept his thoughts to himself. He had learned long ago that it was much safer to act child like around the Padres. The Padres were apt to whip anyone they thought acted too smart.

Working with the cows was pleasant. Estanislao ran to herd them. He had to be careful not to run too fast, or they might panic and stampede. This was very common among tule elk that were very skittish and were very fast runners. He learned from the other Mansos about cows. The mothers were very protective of their young. Mothers would work together to protect their young. Of course, there was nothing to fear in the Mission pastures anyway. The only danger was from grizzly bears. But the soldiers had killed off all the local grizzly bears long ago. There were stories about the soldiers dragging large male grizzly bears out of the hills. This was done very carefully with at least two horsemen holding the bear by ropes so the bear could not charge either rider. The bears were brought down to the Presidio and tied to stakes. They were fed and cared for until a large group of people could be gathered. Then a bull was brought into the area and coaxed to fight the bear. The crowd cheered with each charge of the bull. But, it was inevitable that the grizzly would win the fight. Then both animals would be killed and roasted to feed the crowd.

Estanislao was becoming proficient in Spanish. He was moved to a class where he was taught to read and write. Estanislaa was not allowed to take the class. Women did not need to read and write. They had to raise families for God and Spain. Reading and writing was fascinating to Estanislao. He took to it very quickly. It was like a powerful magic to be able to read what someone else had written. He could even begin to read the Bible and read the word of God for himself. His father had been a messenger for the Laquisimas people. He had been the upstream messenger, living at the eastern end of the village. His job had been to deliver messages of war or other life and death messages. His father had to memorize each message as told to him by the upstream Chief. The Chief created each message after a council of elders meeting to get advice from the elders. His father had to run, up to four hours or more, and deliver the message exactly as told to him. He would then continue on to other villages to deliver the same message. Eventually he returned to the Laquisimas village with the responses from each Chief of the other villages. This could be a long process taking one or two weeks, because each village held a meeting of its elders in order to create their response. But reading and writing were different from simple message delivery. It was more meaningful and even spiritual.

Reading and writing were similar to the use of the Chumash pictographs. Estanislao had visited a painted rock, full of Chumash pictographs, with his father. They had gone in the Spring to ask the Chumash Shaman, called a 'antap (pronounced gontop), about the future. Estanislao's father had been worried about the future, due to changes in the village. The 'antap had asked them to fast and pray with him. He had taken powerful plant preparations and had brought them into the place where the pictographs were found. The 'antap had painted the pictographs on the rock using hematite, charcoal and other pigments. Only the 'antap knew what the pictographs meant. Each pictograph had a different meaning and was used for different purposes. The 'antap had chanted a song in the ceremonial Chumash language, not the regular, spoken language. The song lasted for a long time. Estanislao and his father sat patiently watching as the 'antap passed his hands in front of a pictograph. Eventually as the sun started to set and the light became dim, the pictograph appeared to move. The 'antap seemed to be able to make the pictograph move. When the light was entirely gone, the 'antap took them to the fire circle. They made a fire and talked about what the 'antap saw in the future. Reading was like the pictograph experience. It could make images float in Estanislao's mind, even images of things and places he had never seen before.

As Spring progressed, the cows gave birth and the crops grew high. The Mission had passed

through the winter easily. Estanislao was amazed
that no one had starved to death, and there had
not been many deaths from disease. The Spanish
way was easier than the Yokuts way of life. The
Yokuts stored acorns, dried deer and salmon meat
and little else to survive the winter. Of course,
buckwheat and California holly grew in the late fall
and early winter and could be eaten then. Sugar
bush, lemonade berry, salt bush and a few other
plants provided nourishment in the late fall. But the
Spanish had beans, wheat, corn, fresh meat, milk
and wine during the winter. The Yokuts had wine,
made from elderberries, manzanita berries or holly
leaf cherries. But the Yokut's wine was of limited
quantity and was only drunk during the Spring or
Fall gatherings. They drank the wine to encourage
the men to speak more freely and communicate.
Some of them were not eager communicators and
had to be encouraged. Estanislao had seen the
Padres drink wine and brandy until they were very
drunk and vomited. Only the Yokuts chief and the
Shaman were ever allowed to drink enough wine to
become drunk. Estanislao had never been drunk.
The Laquisimas village Shaman had become
drunk once, in order to induce a sacred dream that
would help him see if the impending war would be
successful.

      The Padres were very happy to see the
progress of the crops and the fattening of the cows.
Estanislao was asked to help keep the ledgers
that recorded the new births among the cows. He
enjoyed this very much and did not mind showing

off his new ability to read and write. Not all of the men were very proficient at reading and writing. Among the Yokuts, knowledge was power. In order to become a Shaman, a man or woman had to pay a high price to go to the Shaman school near Mount Pinos. The price was usually in terms of deer meat, elk hides, pigments, bows, arrows, knives or other valuables. Very few people were rich enough to pay to become Shaman students. All of the Yokuts Chiefs were trained in the Shaman school. They used the knowledge they gained from the school to great advantage with their people. The Chiefs and Shamans knew things that other people did not know about death, the afterlife, magic and evil. This knowledge was sometimes used to frighten people into submitting to the will of the Chief. During gatherings, the knowledgeable ones were allowed into sacred enclosures surrounded by tule hanging mats and feathered banners, that common people could not enter.

Estanislao helped with the crops and the cows. He also got to inspect the irrigation canal every week to make sure it was not clogged. He enjoyed running the entire length of the canal from the Mission to the stream and back. Sometimes Orencio ran with him. Other Mansos sometimes ran with him also. Mostly, Estanislao enjoyed running by himself. It was his time with God. He had formed a very personal relationship with God. He took his Bible study very seriously and worshipped earnestly during church. He prayed every day, sometimes several times. He was

overjoyed to have a God who could be personal
with him. This was unlike the Yokuts beliefs,
where God was not approachable by the common
people. God was aloof and just as likely to harm as
to help. The Yokuts believed that people brought
harm on themselves when they were unworthy,
or had done something wrong. The Yokuts God
punished people frequently, mostly by making them
go hungry. Sometimes the Yokuts God caused
the unworthy to become sick or die. Then it was
said that the person had brought the punishment
on himself. The Spanish God was forgiving and
personal. Estanislao could pray to him, feel
forgiven and comforted. Estanislao had learned to
love God.

        Estanislaa was not as spiritual as
Estanislao. She grumbled about all the work she
was required to do. The Yokuts way had been
easier for her, sometimes. At the Laquisimas
village, she had helped dig roots, pound and
process acorns, process and sew hides, roast
meat, cook and other chores. But she felt more
comradery in the village. There she could be with
the other women, sing, chat and feel at ease while
working. In the Mission, she worked in a room with
a few other women. They were constantly watched
by the Padres to make sure they did their work.
They were not allowed to gossip or sing. They had
to work at the pace set by the Padres. She also
found the work boring. Most of the day, she worked
baking bread. The rest of the day she helped
with sewing. That was her schedule every day.

Sometimes she complained bitterly to Estanislao. She wanted to go home to the village.

Orencia, Estanislao's mother, agreed that life at the Mission was boring. Her job was to make tortillas. Every day, she made the corn dough from corn meal and lime, formed it into tortillas and cooked them on a flat iron pan. But Orencia enjoyed her work. She found it easier than pounding acorns with the heavy pounding stone. She was not particularly interested in gossiping with other women. She had witnessed the perpetuation of too much ill will from gossip. She was more spiritual than Estanislaa, and enjoyed going to Mass. Her Spanish was not as good as other Mansa's, but she continued to work on improving her Spanish.

Sexta was now five years old and enjoyed the Mission. She was becoming very proficient in Spanish. She and the other children all spoke nothing but Spanish. Sexta was being instructed in the Spanish ways. Every day, she went to school to learn how to do things in the Spanish way. She sometimes chided her parents in their lack of knowledge of the Spanish ways. She was very fond of inspecting her parents clothing every day to make sure they were wearing their clothes in the Spanish way. Her father had to have a belt with the shirt tucked into the trousers. Her mother had to have the blouse tucked into the skirt. Sexta did not miss the Laquisimas village, although sometimes she did mention certain friends she had not seen since coming to the Mission.

Quickly, the time came to harvest the spring wheat and plant the summer wheat. Estanislao noticed that the steel head were running in the stream. He brought a few back to the Mission to show the Padres. The Padres said that the fish may be useful to fertilize the corn, but were worthless for eating. Estanislao had eaten steel head many times and knew they tasted good and were very nourishing, but he said nothing. He had also said nothing about the salmon that ran in the fall. The salmon run had not been as abundant as in the river near the Laquisimas village. Every fall, when the salmon ran, the people gathered the fish in large amounts. Of course, so did the grizzly bears. But usually, there were more than enough salmon for the bears and the people. The men had to be careful not to fish where the bears were fishing. The fish died and washed up on the shores in great numbers. Condors, vultures, seagulls, bald eagles and golden eagles came to eat the dead salmon. Estanislao remembered the wonderful salmon roasts in the village. The salmon fillets were roasted by placing them between two forked sticks and leaning them over the fire with many other salmon fillets. There was much singing and dancing in celebration of the salmon. They were always very careful to dance the salmon dance properly. They knew the salmon spirits were watching and judging them, to make sure they were worthy. The Shaman and salmon Chief presided over the gathering and were very keen to judge the salmon dance. The salmon Chief was chosen because of his special ability to predict the salmon run and catch salmon. The Shaman, every year, told the people that God promised the salmon would return next year. This was promised to them, provided they kept the proper balance with nature and were worthy.

Estanislao continued to study diligently and learned new skills. The storage rooms needed to be enlarged. So Estanislao and several other men were recruited to help cut down some local pine trees and saw them into planks. The trees were found in the local hills several miles away. After cutting the trees down they were loaded onto horse carts and hauled back to the Mission. The Padres had large saws that required two or four men to push and pull them. The saws were used to cut down the trees and to saw them into rough planks. The Yokuts had saws made of obsidian mounted in a piece of wood. The saws could be used to cut down small trees, but not the great trees the Spanish saws could cut. One of the soldiers had a father who was a carpenter in Spain. He told the Mansos about how in Spain there are sawmills that cut boards out of logs. The boards are much higher quality than can be made from crude saws. He told the Mansos that someday, the Mission would have its own sawmill and produce fine quality lumber. Then the carpenters would be able to do high quality woodwork. But for now the planks would have to do. They were tied together with raw hide or nailed with nails from Spain. The Mansos quickly constructed the frames for the new rooms.

Then they made adobe from mud, straw and manure. Adobe bricks were made in wooden forms and allowed to dry in the sun. They were put in place and held together with fresh adobe mortar to make the walls. The roof was made of tule reeds, tied to the rafters. The roof was as water proof as any Yokuts house, but was not fire proof.

In August, the Padres told the Mansos to get ready for the ship to come from Spain. The ship would have great surprises from Spain, new cloth, Bibles, nails, food, and other expensive items. The Mansos were told that the ship would return to Spain with hides and tallow from the Mission. This would help pay for the supplies from Spain. The Padres told them this would be the future of the Mission. The Mansos would supply hides and tallow in exchange for food, cloth, Bibles, iron goods and other things that must come from Spain. The Padres told them that they must learn to conduct this business on their own. This would make them good Spanish citizens. Eventually, in thirty years or so, the Mission lands would be turned over to the Mansos. Then, the Mansos would own everything and run everything by themselves. Of course, the Padres would still be there as spiritual leaders.

Estanislao was overwhelmed to hear that one day, the Mansos would own the Mission and all the land. This was very generous of the Spanish, to come here, teach the Mansos the Spanish ways, and give everything to the Mansos. The other Mansos agreed that the Spanish plan was very generous. They looked forward to the day they would be like any other Spaniard. Estanislao remembered the Padre's sermon from many months ago, "God has blessings for everyone."

When the ship arrived, it carried less than Estanislao had imagined. Cloth was delivered, as were nails, food and Bibles, but not the amount that Estanislao had imagined. The Mansos all worked to unload the ship and stack everything on the beach in San Francisco Bay. Then they loaded everything into wagons and hauled all the supplies the long climb from the bay to the Mission. The sailors climbed too. They were treated to a large beef feast at the Mission. The sailors were very keen to get fresh fruit. Estanislao was told that the sailors live on the ship for many months with no fruit. Scurvy could be a common problem among the sailors. Apples and grapes were ready to harvest and were provided to the sailors. The sailors also gathered fresh water for the trip home.

The next day, the real work started. The cows were culled. The cows that were ready, were herded down to the beach. There Estanislao was taught how to hit the cows on the head with a large wooden club. This knocked out the cows. Then the hides and fat were removed from the cows. The hides were processed briefly by scraping them to remove as much fat as possible. Then they were salted and dried in the sun. The fat was taken onto the ship and put into large iron pots, where it was cooked to separate the tallow. The carcasses were pushed out into the bay. Estanislao was upset about the waste of so much meat. He was told there was too much meat to dry it all. He had to agree that as much meat as possible was saved for drying. The carcasses attracted sharks in large numbers, that could be seen eating the carcasses in frenzies. Seagulls, crows and other birds ate the carcasses that washed up on the shore. It was a terrible sight. The water near shore was stained with blood. The carcasses were numerous. The smell of death and decay was prevalent. The sharks and many different kinds of birds were present in large numbers. The Padres were happy. They said this was all God's plan for the Mansos. The Padres said they had ordered large iron pots to render tallow in the Mission, next year. They would be able to save the tallow and process hides themselves in the future. Tallow would be made into candles and soap. For now, all candles and soap came from Spain. Estanislao did not much like the Spanish soap. The Yokuts people made soap out of many different plants that was superior to Spanish soap. The best soap came from the roots of the soap root lily and from the roots of the yucca plant that the Padre's called our Lord's candle.

The work of slaughtering, skinning and hauling hides and fat was exhausting. Estanislao returned at night to the Mission with the other Mansos, but could not bring himself to eat beef. The next day, they got up before the sun and herded more cows down to the ship and started all over. This continued for six days until the Padres figured they had slaughtered enough cows. They would save the rest of the herd to build a bigger herd for next year. They would need more Mansos next year to help with the slaughtering.

Before he knew it, Estanislao had been at the Mission for one year. It was now 1822. He was happy. His family was prospering, although Estanislaa was occasionally bored. He was reading voraciously and learning as much of the Spanish way as possible. His dream was to become a good son of God, citizen of Spain and help Alta California progress. He continued to run to inspect the canal and grew stronger from the work he did at the Mission including the fall harvest work. His runs were about an hour long and were his time with God. As he ran, he asked God questions and frequently felt answers come to him. He especially liked running in the dense fog or the morning darkness, when he felt that he was alone with God.

The winter was a boring time for many Mansos. Nothing to do but sit all day. Estanislao poured himself into his reading all winter long. He was either reading, out running or doing some chores around the Mission. He read everything he could find. He heard that Spain had libraries with hundreds of books. Here at the Mission there were the Bible and a few dozen other books. Of course, he read the Bible every day and memorized the scriptures that he found most important to him. But he was always on the look out for other books. The Padres were amazed at his desire to read. No other Manso was so interested in reading. Estanislao showed clear intelligence and motivation. While most Mansos were bored, Estanislao devoted himself to learning. He found himself thinking that "God has blessings for everyone."

With the Spring came the planting of new crops and birthing of new calfs. The Spring was unusually wet. The rain filled the streams with torrents. Trees were washed into the streams. The hills had several mudslides. This was disastrous for the irrigation canals. The Mansos had to dam the entries to the canals to keep the water from flooding the canals. The dams had to be checked constantly to make sure they were stable. Of course, as the rain continued, the dams eventually broke allowing the canals to flood. This was a terrible time for the Mansos. The fields were flooding with so much water that the new seedlings would drown. The Padres quickly taught the Mansos how to reroute the water so that it flowed out of the fields into the drainage canals. The Mansos also had to use large buckets to bail the water out of the fields into the drainage canals. This was back breaking labor that required many long hours of work. Finally, the fields were emptied of excess water. The dirt had been turned to mud. Many of the seedlings would die, but many others would survive due to the efforts of the Mansos. After that, a strict vigil was kept at the dams to make sure they did not burst again.

While the Mansos were busy bailing

the water away from the fields, a soldier named
Alejandro watched from his perch on top of his
horse. Estanislao heard him laughing at them.
Estanislao asked Alejandro why he was laughing.
Alejandro told him that the stupid Mansos should
use their heads instead of breaking their backs with
all this work. If the Mansos would think about it,
they might come up with a machine to help them do
the work faster and with less effort. Estanislao was
intrigued with this suggestion. He went to Padre
Diego, who was very knowledgeable, and asked
him about a machine to bail water. The Padre
sketched out a large wooden wheel with buckets
attached to the rim. Horses could be used to rotate
the wheel and dip the buckets into the water. As
the wheel rotated, the buckets would rise to the top
and be tipped into the drainage canal. This was
a fascinating idea to Estanislao. Horses could be
used to spare the backs of men and accomplish
the work. Estanislao asked Padre Diego why such
a machine had not been built long ago to use in
an emergency. Padre Diego was very candid with
Estanislao and told him that it was more important
for the Mansos to do the work themselves. It was
important for the Mansos to be kept busy. After all,
a Manso with no work will soon be into mischief.

  The new calfs were growing quickly and
were in need of branding. Some of the Spanish
settlers who lived near the Mission had cattle of
their own. The settlers usually let their cattle graze
with the Mission cattle. That way the Mansos
could watch their cattle for them. The Padres did

not seem to mind that the Mansos did this work for the settlers, without compensation. However, the Padres thought it was important to be able to tell the cows apart. So each settler had a different brand. The Mission brand was a bell shape. Each Mission cow had the brand of the Mission. The Mansos were very good at telling the difference between the cows, even without looking at the brands. They had cared for each cow since it was born and knew each one individually.

Horse hair lariats were made to prepare for the branding. The lariat was a rope that was used to catch the calfs. This involved roping the calf around the hind feet and pulling it to the ground. It took about two weeks to make one lariat by braiding horse hair. There were several lariats from previous seasons, but new lariats were needed in addition since the herd was growing.

The Padres had a surprise for the Mansos this year. Since the herd was so big, the soldiers would not be used to round up the cattle. Instead, some of the Mansos would learn how to ride horses and do the round up themselves. Of course, Rafael, the Alcalde, was chosen to learn how to ride. The Alcalde was the leader of the Mansos. Eleven other Mansos were also chosen to learn how to ride. Estanislao was one of the eleven. Estanislao was thrilled. He found horses fascinating and had wanted to learn how to ride since the first time he saw a horse.

The soldiers had twelve extra horses. These were brought to the Mission with saddles and bridles. The soldiers first taught the twelve Mansos how to saddle and bridle a horse. Then Rafael was told to mount his horse. Rafael put his foot in the stirrup and climbed onto his horse just as the soldiers had shown him. He sat on the horse with a large smile. Estanislao saw that Rafael had also dreamed of riding a horse. Soon it was Estanislao's turn. He climbed into the saddle as if he had ridden before. He was told to use the bridle to tell the horse which way to turn and to kick the horse with his ankles to tell the horse to move. Estanislao made the horse move ahead and turn right. Then he pulled back on the reins to make the horse stop. When he came to a stop, he realized he had held his breath. He exhaled and let out a whoop. He was so happy to feel that large powerful horse move and feel the motion of the saddle. The other Mansos laughed as if to say they had felt the same way when they rode.

Estanislao had much to tell Estanislaa and his mother that night. He described how to put on the saddle and bridle. He told them how he had felt when he got into the saddle. He told them how the muscles of the horse were huge and how he could see the muscles move as the horse walked. He told them how strong and patient the horse was. His family listened intently. Poor Orencio had not been selected to learn to ride. Estanislao assured him that next year, he would be selected to learn. He knew that the Laquisimas people would love to have horses of their own.

The next day, the riding lessons began.

The Mansos were taught how to ride the horses around the corral in a line. On command from the riding master, they turned right or left, or stopped. Several Mansos gathered around to watch the riding lessons. This was great entertainment for them. The riders had to concentrate in order to not make a mistake that would send their audience into riots of laughter. The riding lessons continued for one week. The riding master said the Mansos had learned enough.

Now came the time to break the new horses. Each of the twelve Mansos was given a horse that he would have to break. Rafael was to be the first. He was told to bridle and saddle his horse. This was not easy. Horses do not like taking the bit between their teeth and wearing a bridle. After several minutes, Rafael finally got the bridle on. Putting the saddle on was easier. Then Rafael was instructed to lead the horse by holding the bridle and walking around the corral. The horse did not mind being lead. Rafael talked to him gently. After several minutes of walking, the riding master told Rafael to get on the horse. He said to do it quickly in one movement and hold on to the reins and saddle. Rafael climbed into the saddle in one fluid motion. The horse began to buck immediately. He jumped and circled. Rafael held on well, while all the Mansos laughed in an uproar. Estanislao did not laugh too loud. He knew his time was coming soon. Rafael was bucked from the horse. He sailed through the air and came down on his behind. The riding master told him to get up and do it again. Rafael did as he was told. After being bucked off three times, the horse stopped bucking and let Rafael sit on him. This brought a cheer from the crowd. After some coaxing, the horse learned how respond to the bridle, to turn and stop.

Soon, too soon, it was Estanislao's turn. His horse was a large, black horse that he called Noche. He got up into the saddle in one fluid motion and was on the ground on his back before he knew what had happened. The crowd was howling in laughter. The riding master told Estanislao, "You have a strong horse. He may be too strong for you. I may have to ask one of my soldiers to break him."

Estanislao did not like this insult. He instantly jumped back on the horse and grabbed two handfuls of mane. The animal started to jump and circle violently. The crowd went wild with laughter and cheering. After two circles, Estanislao was bucked off. The horse looked at him with a defiant look as if to ask if that was all he could do. Estanislao did not hesitate to jump back on. The crowd cheered. The horse bucked again, but did not tire. After several bucks and a circle, Estanislao was on the ground. He jumped back on the horse. By now, Estanislao was beginning to feel tired, but did not want to show it. The horse bucked again, as if it were the first time Estanislao had mounted him. Estanislao was amazed at the power of the horse. Soon, he was on the ground. This time the riding master intervened. "No, no. Do not get back on the horse. You may kill him. He is too headstrong. He will buck until he dies. He will not let you ride him today. You may try again tomorrow."

That night, Estanislao had sores and pains all over his body. The powerful horse had really given him a ride. After dinner, he walked slowly and carefully to the stream. He told other people he needed to rest. He was actually interested in getting some willow. He chewed and swallowed a couple of willow leaves, being careful to not let anyone see him. He knew this would help with his aches and pains. He would need all the help he could get before the morning with his aches. He did not want the Padres to see him using a plant they did not approve of.

The next morning, Estanislao saddled and bridled Noche. He jumped on the horse expecting a major battle. The horse did not move. Apparently the horse suffered as much pain as Estanislao. Estanislao let out a whoop. Then he nudged the horse to move ahead. The horse responded and turned when directed with the bridle. Estanislao rode him around the corral for a few minutes, then got off and removed the saddle and bridle.

The next day was the time for the round up. Rafael lead the eleven other riders out to the pasture. The cows ignored them as they rode up. Several soldiers were with them to instruct them in how to separate the new calfs from their mothers. This turned out to be more difficult than Estanislao had anticipated. The mothers were very protective of their young and sometimes stood their ground to protect their calfs. However, a little persistence usually drove the mother away from the calf. The calf was then roped with the lariat. It took a lot of practice to learn how to throw the rope so that it missed the calf's head and body and only caught the hind legs. When the hind legs were roped, the Manso would secure the lariat to the saddle, jump off the horse and tie up the two front legs with a small rope. He would then go to the fire, take out a hot branding iron, bring it to the calf and press the iron to the calf's hide. The hot iron burned the hair and the flesh. The calf cried pathetically. It took practice to learn how long to hold the iron on the hide to get an adequate branding. Rafael became very proficient at roping and branding very quickly. Estanislao competed hard to become as good as Rafael. Some of the soldiers held back and watched. They remarked that Estanislao on his big, black horse was an imposing figure. One soldier was jealous. He had tried to break the horse, with no luck. Another soldier said, "That horse is the devil. Let him take that Indian to hell."

It took several days to brand all the calfs. Estanislao was happy when it was done. He could ride on Noche to inspect the herd and see what he and the other Mansos had accomplished. He was proud of what they had done. One day while inspecting the herd, Rafael came to join Estanislao. Rafael was an Ohlone Indian. He was sixty years old, still very thin and strong. He was a little taller than Estanislao. His people had lived in the canyon near the Mission. His people were the first taken into the Mission by the Padres and soldiers. Estanislao finally got to ask what had happened to the Ohlone people. He had expected to see Ohlone villages in the canyons and hills near the Mission. Rafael told him that at first, the village had continued as before. But eventually, the Mission demanded more Indians to help build the Mission. The Ohlone had come to help and went home to the village at night. Many Ohlone died building the Mission. Construction was difficult and dangerous work. In addition, there had been diseases unknown to the Ohlone, such as the flu, that had killed many people. Many of the teenage girls had developed venereal disease and had not been able to have children. Venereal diseases were rare among the Ohlone, but had become prevalent at the Mission. Rafael told Estanislao that syphilis was brought by the soldiers and the Padres. As Estanislao reacted to this, Rafael quickly hushed him. He said "Do not let anyone know about this. As Alcalde, I know many things that other people do not know."

After the Mission was built, the Padres asked the Ohlone to move their village, called Orisom, nearer to the Mission. The Ohlone had refused. The soldiers had been sent to move the Ohlone village by force. Some Ohlone had been killed. Rafael told Estanislao that this had been the fate of his village and all other Ohlone villages. They had all been taken to work in the Missions. Estanislao asked Rafael when he had been taken to the Mission. Rafael told him that the Mission San Jose had been founded in 1797 by Padre Lasuen. Rafael had been taken to help build the Mission in June and had helped complete the construction. The first church was completed in September. He was about 36 years old at that time. At first, living in the Mission had been pleasant for Rafael and his family. After a few years, Padre Duran and Padre Fortuni had come to take charge of the Mission. Padre Lasuen had moved on, to found other Missions.

Padre Narciso Duran was from Castellon de Ampurias in Catalonia, Spain. He had been born in 1776 and became a Priest in 1792. He volunteered to work in the Indian Missions and went first to Mexico City, then in 1806 to California. He became a very skilled administrator and knew how to cover his tracks. Rafael was most interested in Duran's music. Duran had devised a music system using two note colors and two note shapes so that it would be easier for the Indians to read. He constantly described the Indians as the most stupid of all the American people. Eventually, Duran had an Indian choir and an orchestra whose music he tolerated, although he told them they would never measure up to a Spanish choir or orchestra. Duran always found the Indians to be unruly and were probably better taught by a slave master than a Priest.

Rafael told how his wife had died of the flu after a few years. He had three teenaged children. One of them was a girl, who had died of syphilis.

The other two were boys. One boy had tried to steal a knife from the presidio, where the soldiers lived. He had been beaten for this. He lingered for several days before dying. The other son had stayed at the Mission until he was about 22 years old. He did not want to marry any of the girls, since many of them had venereal diseases. He ran away to the hills and did not return. The soldiers were sent to bring him back, but did not find him. Estanislao was shocked to hear this. He did not understand why anyone would want to run away from the Mission. He enjoyed living at the Mission. Rafael said "He would be about your age now. I have not seen him for many years."

It was sad that Rafael could not find his son. Apparently, he was living with other Indians somewhere. Rafael said "If he is living in another Mission, he has probably changed his name. The Padres really have no way of keeping track of the Indians. There are no papers like the Spanish must have to prove who they are. They don't even give us last names. All the Spanish and Mexicans have two names. The Indians only have one name. Do you know why that is? It is because we are only one third human. Since they think we are two thirds animal, we don't deserve to have last names." Estanislao had heard this before and knew Rafael spoke the truth.

A few days later, Estanislao was out on his morning run to inspect the canal. It was very early. The sun had not come up yet. He saw some men out among the cows, on foot. They quietly lead several calfs away from the herd and into the woods nearby. Estanislao carefully followed them and watched as they branded the calfs with new brands. These settlers were all Spaniards. Estanislao did not dare say anything to them. They all carried guns and would kill him without hesitation if they saw him. He was furious with this injustice and immediately ran to tell the Alcalde. Rafael was still in bed when Estanislao approached his quarters. Rafael lived in an Ohlone style hut by himself. Estanislao entered and gently wakened Rafael. Then he quietly told him that some settlers were in the field branding Mission calfs. Rafael said, "This happens every year. They take a few calfs. We pretend we don't notice. Whatever you do, do not tell the Padres about this." Estanislao knew why he should not tell the Padres. They would beat him for accusing a Spaniard of doing something dishonest. Rafael assured Estanislao that this year, he would get to the bottom of the problem with stealing calfs.

For the next several days, everything continued normally. Estanislao and Orencio helped tend the fields, the cows and the canal. Estanislaa and Orencia helped with the cooking and the sowing. Sexta continued to become a perfect little Spanish girl. Estanislao had to be careful with her. Sometimes Sexta would run to Padre Jose and tell him if her father did something that was not appropriate for a Spaniard, such as singing a Yokuts song while he worked. This could cost Estanislao a lashing.

One night as Estanislao slept, he felt a cold hand grab his arm. He started to cry out, but another hand was clamped over his mouth. As he awoke, he realized it was Rafael. He looked at Rafael in the dark and realized he was suffering. Estanislao quickly got up, grasped Rafael around the shoulders and hauled him out of the hut. The two men quietly walked away from the other huts so they could speak without being heard. Rafael was openly bleeding from a large gash on his left side. Estanislao knew the best way to stop bleeding was to apply pressure with his hands. When he did this, Rafael nearly fell over with pain. He said, "Do not try to stop the bleeding. It is too late anyway. I must tell you that I have found out about the stealing of calfs. Padre Duran sells the calfs to the settlers without telling us. I saw him with some settlers tonight. He sold the calfs for about half what they are worth. I assume he keeps the money for himself and not the Mission. Otherwise, he would do the business during the day and tell us about it. One of the settlers heard me hiding in a bush. He did not see me, but he stabbed into the bush with his sword. Just my luck, he got me. You must take my body to the canal and throw me in. That way my body can be carried to the bay. No one will find my body. No one will figure out that I know about the stealing of calfs."

Estanislao said "No. I will take you to my mother. She knows many Yokuts remedies and can help you survive. We can hide you in the hills." Rafael was now becoming very weak from all the blood he had lost. Estanislao saw that he would not live much longer. Rafael fainted. Estanislao realized it was not a good idea to take Rafael to his mother. Instead, he hoisted Rafael on his back and carried him across the field to the canal. By the time they got to the canal, Rafael was no longer breathing. Estanislao put the body in the canal and watched as it was swept away by the water. He carefully washed Rafael's blood off his back and arms. He paused to say a prayer for Rafael. Then he went back to bed. It was impossible for him to sleep knowing that Padre Duran was betraying the Mission this way. He kept wondering what would happen if he told Padre Fortuni about this. The two Padres shared leading the Mission. Surely, Fortuni would help with this situation. But he knew that if he mentioned anything to Fortuni, he would be beaten. Estanislao found himself thinking about Duran, "God has blessings for those who help themselves."

The next morning, the call went out to find Rafael. The soldiers assumed he had run away to the hills like his son. The Padres were sure that Rafael would not run away. He was a good son of Spain. He had been Alcalde for several years and was very trusted. The Mansos were kept in the Mission grounds while the soldiers searched for Rafael. At lunch time, the soldiers returned without Rafael. The garrison leader, Capitan Rodriguez, gave a report to the Padres. "After searching for several hours, we found a few threads hanging on a bush on the western side of the fields. I assume that Rafael has been abducted by hostile Indians. I want to lead a party to go after the Indians and get Rafael back." Estanislao knew that Rafael had not been on the western side of the fields. He had been on the southern side, near the settlers. He had placed Rafael's body in the canal on the southern side of the fields.

Padre Fortuni said "Capitan, please lead your men on a search for these Indians and punish them. Then bring back Rafael to us." The soldiers mounted a campaign of twenty five men, each armed with guns and swords. They rode out that afternoon. Estanislao marveled at the campaign. They were slow and cumbersome. They hauled a wagon of provisions with them. The wagon moved slowly. Surely, the soldiers could move much faster if they left the wagon behind and just carried light provisions with them. They could hunt, fish and gather food as they needed it. It also was a shock to Estanislao how arrogant the soldiers were. They rode out with confidence that they could slaughter any Indians they met. This was not the Yokuts way. Among his people, they would have prayed all night in preparation for battle. The next morning they would have bathed to purify themselves. The Shaman would bless them to give them strength. Then they would go out to battle. The soldiers had simply gotten their kits together, been blessed by the Padre and ridden off singing and laughing.

The soldiers were gone for nearly two weeks. When they returned they shouted about their triumph before they got to the Mission. They wanted everyone to hear that they had killed some Indians. As they rode up to the Mission, they threw two heads on the ground. They were the heads of adult, male Indians. The Captain gave his report. "We found these two hiding in the bushes as we rode by. They had bows and arrows. We caught them and questioned them. It seems neither of them spoke any Spanish. Unfortunately, they died during interrogation. We brought their heads back as proof." Padre Duran was furious. "You will not bring heads back to the Mission again. We will take your word for it that you found some Indians in the future. Now get them out of my sight." There was no mention of Rafael.

The next morning, Padre Duran called Estanislao into his office. The office was a small cubicle decorated with a small crucifix and lighted by a large candle. "Estanislao, I have noticed that your Spanish is improving. I also hear that you read Spanish and can even write." Estanislao told him that he had read several books in Spanish. The Padre was astonished. "I do not believe that an Indian can read and understand an entire book in Spanish. But you may have been able to skim through the pages and get some rudimentary understanding." Estanislao was not surprised to hear the Padre say this. Padre Duran was famous for underestimating the Indians. It seemed to stem from his desire to teach them to sing. Padre Duran had adapted a color coded system of music from the Mission San Juan Bautista. Each note was a different color or shape depending on whether it was do, ray, mi and so on. After much effort, he had successfully taught the Mansos to read the music and sing a song. He did not understand that the Indian musical staff was pentatonic, not based on the octave. After several years, many of the Mansos had become proficient singers. Still Padre Duran insisted that they sang like cows suffering from stomach aches.

Padre Duran tested Estanislao by writing a paragraph of instructions about reaping a field of wheat. Estanislao read the passage aloud and answered detailed questions about what it meant. Padre Duran said, "Well, I guess you understand a few things. But you will never understand Spanish like a Spaniard." The day continued with more tests. Estanislao had to make a ledger and fill it in with items needed for the upcoming harvest. This was a long task that took nearly three hours. The Padre returned to look at the ledger. "You have done a barely adequate job. There are several mistakes and omissions. I guess you aren't as clever as you think you are."

That evening after dinner, instead of going to classes, Padre Fortuni called Estanislao to his office. He said "Estanislao, you are being considered for a new job. This job requires great honesty. Do you believe that it is important to be honest?" Estanislao assured him that honesty is very important. The Padre went on to say "Several calfs have gone missing from the heard. When I asked Rafael about this, he meerly said he did not know what had happened to them. Do you know what happened to them?" Estanislao was now on edge, but he knew he had to speak carefully. "I can look into the situation for you." The Padre said "Are you sure you don't know anything about this? Several soldiers have suggested that the Mansos are selling the calfs to the settlers. The soldiers even claim they can recognize some Mission calfs in the settlers herds." Estanislao said "This is a job for the soldiers. I do not dare go near the settlers' herds. They would kill me." Padre Fortuni said "True. You seem to understand the problem. It may be best for me to ask the Capitan to look into this problem." He and Estanislao had a long conversation about the Bible and which scriptures Estanislao liked best. Estanislao told him that his favorite part of the Bible is the sermon on the mount where Jesus preached to many people with great humility and wisdom. The Padre said "Yes. That is a very simple part of the Bible that many people like. Yet it is a very pleasing passage that even I enjoy reading." After a couple hours the Padre said "I am pleased that you seem to understand the Bible so well. I assume that Padre Jose has been very successful at teaching you the scriptures. Still you have been a good student. Please report to Padre Duran tomorrow morning. You will be the new Alcalde."

Estanislao 3. Estanislao learns the Spanish ways

Estanislao was overwhelmed with his new job, Alcalde. It was 1823. He had so many new responsibilities. He had to make sure the cows were properly cared for, the fields were tended, the canal brought water, the buildings were kept in repair, each man and woman had a job and were trained to do the job and other responsibilities. He was also the peace keeper among the Mansos. This meant that he heard all the gossip. His most difficult responsibility was keeping the Mansos away from the soldiers and the settlers. There was nothing but trouble for a Manso or Mansa almost anytime they encountered a Spaniard or Mexican. Most of all, Estanislao worked very hard at keeping himself from not becoming personally involved in the various squabbles. Estanislaa was very happy that her husband was now Alcalde. This gave her more respectability among the Mansas and made it possible for her to go home with her husband to visit their Laquisimas people. Visits by Mansos to their former villages was forbidden, except for certain privileged people such as the Alcalde and other trusted Mansos. Estanislao discussed this with Estanislaa and decided that as soon as possible, he would find a way for them to go visit their families and friends.

Sexta was now the most popular child in the Mission. Her father was Alcalde. That meant she would have special privileges. She might even be given special gifts from Spain. No other girl her age had anything that was actually from Spain, except for soap. She repeatedly asked her father for some combs for her hair from Spain, so she could look just like a real Spanish lady. Estanislao each time promised her he would ask Padre Duran about combs from Spain for her hair. But he knew that such combs would become the envy of every woman in the Mission. Such an elaborate gift would cause too much envy.

Estanislao worked very hard in the fields every day and carefully made sure all the ledgers were kept of the crops, the 10,000 cows, the 8,000 horses, the 10,000 sheep, the buildings and the tools. He supervised all the Mansos and Mansas, about 1,800 total. He worked everyday with the Padres, especially Padre Duran who was very interested in keeping track of the ledgers. Whenever he was with the Padres he was very careful to be very respectful and never encourage their anger. Padre Duran was very quick to anger, but did not usually administer lashes. This task he delegated to Padre Jose.

Finally, Estanislaa had some good news. She was pregnant. She was very happy. In fact, her belly was already growing. She had suspected for awhile that she was pregnant, but had waited until her belly grew to tell others. Orencia was also very pleased that another grandchild was on the way. Estanislao was proud that he was helping to expand the Mission population. Orencia said that according to Yokuts traditions, the child would be born in December.

Estanislao went to Padre Fortuni the next morning to tell him the good news and to ask for a two week vacation to visit his people on the Laquisimas River. Padre Fortuni was pleased and granted him and his family a vacation. Estanislao was puzzled by something the Padre said. "I won't have the soldiers go with you this time. You need to go tomorrow. There isn't enough time to organize the soldiers to escort you." Estanislao felt safe going on his own and did not want soldiers to go with him. The family, including his brother Orencio, spent the day preparing to walk back to Laquisimas. The walk would take about 5 days. They needed provisions for the walk. They would spend about 5 days visiting their friends and relatives, then walk back to the Mission. To haul their provisions, the Padre had granted them the use of Noche, the big, black horse.

The next day, Estanislao, Estanislaa, Sexta, Orencia and Orencio left the Mission. They walked up the canyon to the top of the hills, down the other side, past Laguna Blanca and across the San Joaquin Valley to the Laquisimas River. They had already been walking for 4 days. They had walked from sunrise to past sunset everyday. Estanislao was very happy to be out traveling. They had to take many breaks for Sexta, who was only 5 years old. Finally, they saw a Yokuts messenger running along the river. They asked him where the Laquisimas people were. He told them to continue up the river to the place where the geese come in the Fall. Estanislao knew the place. They would be there before dark.

When they got to their village, some people and relatives greeted them and were very happy to see them. Others were more guarded about greeting them. It was already night time. A large fire was built and everyone was invited to hear their stories about the Spanish. Poor Sexta developed a fever and went to bed early. She had not spoken Yokuts for over a year and felt more comfortable speaking Spanish anyway. Orencia and Estanislaa told their stories of the Mission until late at night. Estanislao and Orencio were allowed to speak occasionally also.

The next day, they dressed in traditional Yokuts clothing and joined the village. Estanislao was anxious to go out fishing with the men, so he could tell them about the Spanish fighting techniques. Of course, his horse, Noche, was the talk of the village. A messenger was sent out to tell neighboring villages about the horse, so they could come and see. They had seen horses before. But this was the first horse that a Yokuts had brought. All previous horses had been ridden by Spanish.

One of the braves, Lancut, came to Estanislao and said "It is good that the soldiers did not come with you. When Pedro came to visit the last time, there were 10 soldiers with him, and a cannon. The soldiers took 5 children and 3 women with them when they left. I know I can tell you this without making you angry with me." Estanislao was shocked to hear this. The real purpose of the soldier escort for Mansos on vacation was to abduct new converts for the Mission. Lancut said "You can see how few of us there are left now. Our village used to be 400 people. Now we are only 25."

That evening, Sexta developed a cough. By the next morning her lungs were congested. The Healer came to treat her. The Healer prayed for her and gave her a preparation of yerba santa. He also gave her some willow leaves to chew for her fever. She felt better the next morning. But still had congestion in her lungs.

The days passed too quickly. Estanislaa was so happy to see her relatives and show them her growing belly. Orencia was happy too and did not look forward to the long walk back to the Mission. As they left the village, the people all gathered to sing them a blessing for a safe journey. They started back with poor Sexta still coughing. Estanislao had to carry her for most of the afternoon. That night, they camped beside the river. Sexta developed more lung congestion and her fever rose. Orencio was sent back to the village to get the Healer. By morning, Sexta was dead. Estanislao, Estanislaa and Orencia grieved for her. They sang a Christian song over her grave marked with a small cross made from two branches. At lunchtime, Orencio returned to say the Healer was on his way, but found that it was too late. They stayed by the grave until morning when the Healer came. The Healer sang the traditional songs for the departed.

Estanislao missed Sexta, his little girl. She had been a source of pride and joy for him. He got down on his knees and prayed to ask God why Sexta had been taken from them. He felt no answer, but praying comforted him. He asked the Healer why children die. The Healer said "God takes them. That is the way it has always been. Do not grieve, you can have more children. Your wife is already pregnant. Think of the future, not the past." Estanislao began to understand that God is not easy. God's ways are not simple.

When they returned to the Mission, it was comforting to see that it was just as they had left it. Estanislao reported to Padre Duran and told him of the passing of Sexta. Duran promised to pray for her at Mass. Then Duran wanted a full report of how many Yokuts people they had seen, where they were, were they receptive to the Spanish and many other questions.

By now, Mission San Jose was becoming one of the most prosperous Missions in California. Padre Duran took great joy in this prosperity. Padre Fortuni paid more attention to spiritual matters. The summer harvest was bountiful and required more storage rooms than ever before. New storage rooms had to be built quickly. That meant taking long trips to find pine trees, cut them down and haul them back to the Mission. The closest pine trees were more than half a day's walk. Hauling them back in horse drawn wagons required another day. Once the rooms were built, and the harvest stored, then came the never ending vigil to keep the rats out of the harvest.

The sheep flock was now enormous and required many days of shearing to remove all the wool. Padre Duran told Estanislao that this year he would allow some Spanish settlers to help with the shearing. The settlers would of course be able to keep a reasonable portion of what they sheared. Estanislao was not happy with this situation, but had to agree that there was more than enough work for the Mansos. Even the Mansas were recruited to help with the shearing.

During the shearing, no one was left to watch the cattle. That night, several calfs disappeared. Estanislao knew they could be found in the settler's herds. He also knew that if he went to get them, the Spanish would accuse him of stealing their calfs. The soldiers would come. He would be beaten. As tired as they were from shearing, every night at least 4 Mansos had to watch the cows.

Estanislao went to Padre Fortuni for help. "Padre, there are more than 10,000 cows, 8,000 horses and 10,000 sheep. There are also many acres of wheat, grapes, corn, vegetables and a canal to water them. Just keeping the ledgers for the animals alone is a full time job. When harvest time comes, it will be impossible to keep ledgers for the harvest and the animals at the same time."

Fortuni smiled and agreed. "Yes the job of alcalde has become very big. I have been thinking that we may need two alcaldes or more. Perhaps, one alcalde for the animals and one for the crops. I will discuss this with Padre Duran."

Within a week another alcalde was appointed to mind the fields, named Narciso. He was a Yokuts from the Mokelumne people. He was two years younger than Estanislao and had worked tending the fields at the Mission for the past 3 years. Like Estanislao, he had voluntarily come to the Mission after one of his family, his 12 year old sister, was taken to the Mission.

Narciso was about 6 feet 2 inches tall, two inches taller than Estanislao. He had very big shoulders and arms from plowing, planting, weeding, harvesting and the other farm chores. He was one of the strongest men in the Mission. Like Estanislao, he had a very personal relationship with God and was very spiritual. Unfortunately, he did not read and write as well as Estanislao. He would have to be trained to keep the ledgers properly. Estanislao worked diligently with Narciso every night for two weeks until he was confident Narciso could keep the ledgers.

The year passed as the previous years had, except that Estanislaa grew bigger every month. She finally delivered a healthy little boy in December of 1823. She named him Estanislao. Padre Duran immediately started referring to him as Junior. Estanislao and his family passed a happy winter. He finally had some time to return to reading. Of course, the baby kept him up at night for the first two months.

In the Winter of 1824 came the shocking news from the south. Some Mansos had revolted against the Missions and had destroyed some Mission buildings and killed some innocent people. Padre Duran made the announcement during siesta. On Sunday, February 21 some Mansos at the Mission Santa Inez had gone crazy. They had shot their bows and arrows at innocent people. They had burned and destroyed the Mission. The Padre was sorry that only two of Mansos had been killed. Then they fled to the Mission La Purisima Concepcion. The crazy Mansos had entirely taken over La Purisima and had converted it into a fort. Some of the Mansos had gone to the Mission Santa Barbara, had destroyed some structures and tried to get the Mansos there to join the rebellion. At La Purisima, two innocent travelers were killed, by the Mansos, while walking on the road. The Mansos had fought against the Mexican Army, but had eventually lost because they were just Indians and did not know how to fight. This was the first time Estanislao had heard of the Mexican Army and did not know why they had authority. The Padre was happy that 16 of the Mansos had been killed and 7 were sentenced to death. Padre Duran was sure that the devil had taken over the Mansos and caused them to do this evil. He was glad that in the end, God's will was done and the evil ones were punished.

Over the next few days, rumors were heard

among the Mansos about the revolt. The Chumash
in Mission Santa Inez were unhappy because
they had to pay the salaries of the soldiers at the
Mission. The soldiers were supposed to protect
them. Instead the soldiers were cruel to them.
The Chumash felt that the Spanish had promised
in 1786 when the Chumash built the Mission, that
the Missions would be given to the Indians in 30
years. That 30 years was now past. The Chumash
wanted their land back and the Missions they had
built. There was a problem with this however. The
Spanish colony called New Spain had declared its
independence from Spain in 1810 and changed its
name to Mexico. Since the Mexicans quickly took
possession of California, the Spanish promises
were no longer important. Estanislao was surprised
by this news. Why had the Padres and the soldiers
continued to stay at the Mission if it was now
Mexican property? Why did the Padres pretend
they were still training the Mansos to become
Spanish?

After hearing these rumors, Estanislao took
more notice of some of the expenses in his ledgers.
He asked Padre Duran why the salaries of the
soldiers appeared as expenses in the ledgers. The
Padre said, "Estanislao, you and your people need
protection from hostile Indians. Mexico cannot
afford to pay the soldiers. Spain certainly will not
pay them. It makes sense for the Mansos to pay
for their own protection."

The Manso network eventually passed,
by word of mouth, the story of what had happened

among the Chumash at the Mission Santa Ines.
A comet had been visible in the night sky during
February of 1824. Some Chumash took this as an
omen of possible changes. Then, in late February,
a Manso had been flogged at the Mission Santa
Ines. The other Mansos felt he had not deserved
the flogging. On the afternoon of February 21,
1824, the Mansos revolted. They burned the
Mission and the soldier's quarters. Two Chumash
were killed. Several soldiers were wounded, but
Padre Uria was spared by the Chumash. Later
that day, the Mansos (Chumash) at the nearby
Mission La Purisima heard about the revolt, armed
themselves with bows and arrows and took over
the Mission. The six soldiers at the Mission quickly
surrendered. The soldiers accused the Mansos
of killing four Mexican travelers who were passing
by the Mission. The Mansos at La Purisima were
lead by a Chumash man named Pacomio. Not far
away, at the Mission Santa Barbara, the Mansos
(Chumash) were afraid the soldiers would attack
them during mass. So they armed themselves
for battle. The women and children were sent up
Mission Creek to hide. About 300 Chumash men
waited for battle. The battle lasted three hours
and ended in a standoff when Captain Jose De
la Guerra retired his troops to the presidio. This
left the mission in the control of the Mansos. Four
soldiers had been wounded. Three Chumash had
been killed. The next day, the Mansos fled into the
hills.

      The story continued that soldiers had been

sent to hunt down the Mansos from Santa Barbara. The soldiers killed any Indian they found and burned any Indian house they found. They killed four Chumash from Dos Pueblos who had not been involved in the revolt. The runaways continued running to the San Joaquin Valley near Tulare Lake, where they joined other refugees from Santa Ines and La Purisima. Lieutenant Narciso Fabregat was ordered to take 80 men and bring back the runaways, who numbered several hundred. On April 9, Fabregat found some of the runaways to the south near Buena Vista Lake. He chased these Indians south into the San Emigdio Hills at the base of Mount Pinos, where he and Sargeant Carlos Carrillo killed four Indians. At this point, Fabregat declared his victory and returned to Santa Barbara.

At the same time, in late March, 100 soldiers were sent to La Purisima. The Mansos had occupied the Mission for a month. This battle ended in a stand off, until Padre Antonio Rodriguez convinced the Mansos to surrender. Among the Mansos, 16 were dead and several were wounded. The official report indicated that one soldier was killed and two were wounded in the battle. The Mansos counted many more dead soldiers than the report indicated. The soldiers condemned 7 Mansos to death and 12 to long prison terms for their parts in the revolt.

Commandante De la Guerra convinced Governor Arguello to send another envoy to bring back the runaways at San Emigdio. On June 2, 1824 Captain Pablo de la Portilla lead 62 soldiers from Santa Barbara. They were joined by 60 soldiers from Monterey. Both groups of soldiers had cannons and were ready for battle. Padre Vicente de Sarria and Padre Ripoll accompanied the expedition. Padre de Sarria thought the Chumash could be convinced to surrender if they were offered a pardon. He had convinced Governor Arguello to issue a pardon. Capitan de la Portilla carried the pardon with him. Padre de Sarria and Padre Ripoll met with the Chumash in San Emigdio and after much debate were able to convince many of them to return to the Mission, without bloodshed. Over one third of the runaways chose to not return to the Missions and stayed in the San Joaquin Valley. Of course, the soldiers were never punished for killing innocent Chumash or for burning Chumash homes.

A few days later, an envoy came to San Jose from the Mission Santa Barbara. The message carried was a letter appointing Padre Duran as the new Padre Presidente of the Mission system. This was a real honor for Padre Duran and for the Mission San Jose. This honor usually went to the Padre with the most financially successful Mission. Padre Duran was also a skilled politician who knew how to keep his superiors happy and his peers envious. Padre Duran had been at the Mission San Jose since 1806 and was beginning to feel like it was his turn to have some honors. Padre Fortuni had come to the Mission San Jose at the same time as Duran, but had no such aspirations. The appointment as Padre Presidente was a three year title. He would be able to conduct his business from the Mission San Jose, but would also have to travel to other Missions frequently. Travel would give him more opportunities to improve his political position.

Estanislao had a new status with the soldiers. Not only was he Alcalde, but he also had been the only one who could break Noche. Even now, few Spanish tried to ride Noche. The horse had become loyal to Estanislao. The new Capitan, Alejandro, frequently invited Estanislao to join the soldiers in the presidio for lunch. Alejandro wanted to train Estanislao to control the Mansos better in case there was ever a riot. Of course, Narciso would be trained also. The soldiers were nervous about Manso uprisings because of the Chumash uprisings at the Missions Santa Inez, La Purisima Concepcion and Santa Barbara. Alejandro had found out that the Chumash leader was named Pacomio. Apparently, Pacomio had escaped after the rebellion. Alejandro and the other soldiers were afraid that Pacomio might try to cause trouble at other Missions.

Estanislao and Narciso joined the soldiers at lunch time most days and worked through siesta learning how to control crowds. They learned how to use knifes and swords. They learned how to ride a horse into battle. They learned about armor. The soldiers used a vest made of thick leather. This was adequate to stop most Indian arrows, since the arrows were very light. One old Spanish soldier, near retirement age, told Estanislao

"Someday these Indians will figure out that all they have to do is use a good strong wood like oak to make an arrow. Then their arrows will go right through our leather vests." The soldier's name was Pepe. Pepe told Estanislao many things. He even told Estanislao that when he retired to Spain, he would have his own big house with a veranda overlooking Madrid. He would live a comfortable life. Estanislao was surprised to hear that the salaries paid the soldiers by the Mansos could buy so much in Spain. Estanislao asked Pepe "Why do the Padres pretend that California is still part of Spain, not Mexico?" Pepe told him "The Padres live in their own spiritual world and don't want to worry about political things." Estanislao asked Pepe about the Padres retirement and what the Padres could expect from retirement. Pepe said "Don't worry about the Padres. They will do much better than me when they retire."

Estanislao found two books on military techniques in the soldier's library. He borrowed them and studied them thoroughly. He learned about marching into battle, surrounding an enemy, cutting off the enemy retreat, how to use cannons effectively and many other things. He was amazed at the power of cannons. They could blow holes in thick walls and could kill many people with each shot. He longed to be trained in how to shoot a gun and a cannon. But Capitan Alejandro was not interested in training him with guns and cannons. Estanislao watched very carefully whenever a soldier loaded and shot a gun or a cannon. He would ask Pepe a question or two to find out more, such as "What is that black powder they pour in the guns? What are the bullets and cannon balls made of? How do you aim a gun or a cannon?" Pepe was very talkative about these matters and told Estanislao everything he needed to know. After all, what would happen if Estanislao needed to quickly dispel an angry crowd attacking one of the Padres? A gun would be necessary.

One day when Capitan Alejandro was away, Pepe took Estanislao to the soldier's barn. He brought a rifle along. In the barn, where no one could see, Pepe showed Estanislao how to load a gun. He did not allow Estanislao to use gun powder. But Estanislao now knew how to load a muzzle loaded gun. Estanislao tried not to let on how excited he was to actually be able to hold and aim a gun. He forced his hands to not tremble. Afterward, he nonchalantly handed the gun back to Pepe and with an air of disinterest said "Thank you."

That night Capitan Alejandro returned from the Mission Santa Clara. Estanislao walked to the presidio to return a book. As he left the presidio, he noticed a Mansa walking along the road. He went to her and introduced himself. She recognized Estanislao, but he did not recognize her. Her name was Maria. She was 16 years old and from the Laquisumne people. She had been brought to the Mission at the same time as Orencio. Estanislao noticed that she was wearing a fine necklace with a crucifix, probably from Spain. He asked her where

93

she got the necklace. Maria replied that someone had given it to her and would not say who. Such a gift could only come from someone with money to pay for such an expensive item. Estanislao asked her why she was out alone late at night. Maria replied that she was running an errand for Padre Jose who had asked her to bring some towels to the presidio.

The next day, Estanislao noticed that there were other teenage girls who had fancy necklaces, like Maria's. In fact, there were quite a few fancy necklaces to be seen. A week later, he was called to a Manso's hut. Inside he found a teenage girl with a fever and a very tender lower abdomen. Her mother said that the girl had bled when she urinated. The parents were upset. They had also called in Orencia, who knew something about healing. Orencia had seen the disease before. It was an uncommon disease in Laquisimas that was caused by having sex with the wrong person. After some discussion, Estanislao realized he had read something about this disease. It is called gonorrhea. Orencia went to get some yerba mansa for the girl. The yerba mansa would cure the disease in a few days. As Estanislao was preparing to leave the hut, he noticed a fancy, Spanish necklace hanging on the wall. He asked the girl where she got the necklace. She said that Capitan Alejandro had given it to her.

The next day, Estanislao had a talk with his mother. He asked her how many cases of gonorrhea she had seen in the Mission. She said that many of the teenage girls got either gonorrhea or the other disease called syphilis. He asked her if she knew how they were getting these diseases. Orencia said "Usually one of the soldiers offers them a pretty necklace from Spain. Of course, Padre Jose sometimes gives out Spanish necklaces also." Estanislao did not worry much about these sexually transmitted diseases. Yerba mansa cured them. But he resolved to ask Padre Fortuni to mention during one of his sermons that teenage girls should abstain from sex before marriage.

The next few days were occupied with military campaigns by the soldiers. Soldiers from the Mission San Francisco had come to participate in military games. The soldiers formed teams and engaged in mock battles against each other. Estanislao watched as they charged across the fields on their horses attacking each other. He observed all the military tactics he had read about. At dinner time each day, he had a talk with Pepe about what he had observed during the day.

Pepe enjoyed bragging about his military exploits. He told Estanislao about how in 1798 he had gone to a creek in the hills not too far from Laquisimas. The people who lived there were the Miumne. Padre Lasuen had ordered that more converts were needed for the new Mission. Padre Pedro Munoz had been along with the soldiers to talk to the Indians. The Yokuts people were unreceptive to the idea of going to the Mission. Padre Munoz had learned a few words of Yokuts and asked the Miumne people to return the next year, or ray steem ba in Yokuts. This literally means "we will meet here again." After that, the creek was called Orestimba. The next year Padre Munoz and the soldiers returned. The Miumne were again not interested in going to the Mission. The soldiers were ordered to take the children and tie them onto a rope by the thumbs. The Miumne men fought hard to free their children. The soldiers shot the men as they charged. The men continued to charge even in the face of certain death. Pepe had to chuckle as he thought of all those Yokuts men charging at the soldiers only to be easily shot. Pepe said "I guess we killed about 150 men that day. I personally killed about 20. I have never seen anybody so willing to die as those men. But we brought about 70 children back to the Mission on that trip."

Estanislao had heard this story from the Yokuts point of view. How the Spaniards had viciously abducted so many children and had slaughtered so many men while laughing at the men they killed. Of course, the women who survived had followed their children to the Mission, while grieving for their men. Estanislao asked Pepe if the Padre had forgiven them for their carnage. Pepe said "Padre Munoz swore us all to secrecy. He did not want anyone to know how we got those children. But by following Padre Munoz' way of getting converts, the Mission San Jose got the most converts of any northern Mission."

Estanislao knew that this one battle had

wiped out the Miumne people. Those who were not killed or abducted, scattered to live with other Yokuts people. The Miumne had numbered about 300 people at one time. Estanislao asked "Who was the military leader of the soldiers?" Pepe said "Gabriel Moraga. Capitan Moraga, is one of the best soldiers in all of California. He is afraid of nothing and can defeat anyone. Of course, he is old and retired now."

Pepe continued by talking about the Chumash Pacomio. "This Pacomio doesn't know anything about fighting. All he can do is hide behind a Mission wall and shoot bows and arrows. His arrows don't hurt anyone. He doesn't know any tactics at all. He even got ahold of two cannons, but couldn't shoot them straight. He did more harm to himself than to the soldiers with those cannons. The soldiers only needed 3 hours to defeat him in battle." Pepe then leaned closer to Estanislao. "In fact, in all of California, there has only been one smart battle fought by the Indians. It was down by Mission San Diego several years ago. The soldiers were out trying to catch some Mansos who ran away from the Mission. There were a bunch of Indians hiding in the bushes and in holes in the ground. As the soldiers approached, the Indians jumped up with long lances. They stabbed all the soldiers. Killed all of them. It took awhile for anyone to figure out how they did it. They had used some of those our lord's candle stems as lances." Estanislao knew the plant, a yucca plant, that his people used for food, soap, fiber and to make sandals. Deep inside, he was happy to hear that the Spanish could be defeated. The soldiers were arrogant with their guns and horses. They thought they could easily defeat any Indian enemy. He kept his thoughts to himself.

His work kept him very busy. But eventually, he had a talk with Padre Fortuni about gonorrhea and syphilis among the teenage girls. He told the Padre that many of the girls were afflicted with these diseases. He also informed the Padre that when they married, they passed the diseases to their husbands. He did not tell the Padre that it was clear the diseases were coming from the soldiers and some of the Padres.

The Padre looked sad and said, "Yes. I have known about this for some time. It is very unfortunate. I have read the opinion of a Doctor in Spain who thinks that gonorrhea decreases the fertility of women. I have worried that the low birth rate we see here at the Mission is due to this problem. I am very sad that other than you and your wife, there are very few couples who have produced children recently. Unfortunately, these girls have made the decision to give their favors to the wrong men. It is the will of God that they have these problems."

Clearly, the Padre did not know that these wrong men were all Spaniards and Mexicans. Estanislao asked him to consider discussing this issue in a future mass. The Padre did not enjoy being told what to preach by a Manso, and told Estanislao to keep his advice to himself. However, about a week later, the Padre did talk about the importance of abstaining from sex until after marriage.

Estanislao asked his mother to talk to each young couple having trouble with fertility and find out if the wife had suffered from gonorrhea. About a week later, Orencia gave him the news that each of the young women who could not conceive admitted to having suffered from gonorrhea before marriage. Most of them had been cured with yerba mansa. Orencia guessed that something about the disease made young women infertile. The most disturbing news was that nearly one half of the 200 young wives were infertile.

Estanislao and Narciso worked well together. But Estanislao did not entirely trust Narciso because he had come from the Mokelumne people. His people were neighbors and enemies of the Laquisumne people of Laquisimas. The Mokelumne were lead by Chief Te-mi, who had great political power among several tribes of Yokuts people. One day, while working together clearing brush from the canal, Estanislao confronted Narciso. "You are from the Mokelumne people, do you think of yourself as my enemy? I am from the Laquisumne." Narciso did not look up from his work. "I am Miumne. My family were taken prisoner by the Mokelumne." Estanislao understood immediately, "After the massacre at Orestimba Creek, your family escaped and were taken prisoner by the Mokelumne?" Narciso said "Yes. I am not your enemy, Estanislao. I would rather work with you and not against you."

The Fall of 1825, Estanislao Junior, now less than 2 years old developed a high fever. Orencia came quickly to help. The baby had congestion in his lungs and coughed frequently. Orencia gave him a decoction of yerba santa. She carefully dripped it from her finger into his mouth, one drop at a time. The baby did not hold the medicine down. He vomited after every dose of yerba santa. Estanislaa stayed up all night caring for her son. The next evening, when Estanislao returned home from work, Estanislaa sat grieving. Their son had died during the day of pneumonia. Estanislao sat and grieved with his wife. They sang a Christian song for their boy.

Padre Fortuni was overtaken by grief with the news of the death of the baby. Estanislao was surprised to see so much emotion from the Padre. Apparently, he was very concerned about the low birth rate at the Mission and the low numbers of children at the Mission. A funeral was organized for that evening. They lit candles and marched to the cemetery not far from the Mission. As his son was buried, Estanislao looked around the cemetery as if seeing it for the first time. He realized how big the cemetery was. There must be many hundreds of Mansos buried here. All the graves of Mansos were unmarked.

That winter, the flu hit hard at the Mission. Several hundred Mansos died of the flu. Fortunately, Orencia had collected some elderberry blossoms during the summer. As the flu ravaged

100

the Mission, she brewed a tea of elderberry blossoms to give her family. They all survived the winter. Estanislaa contracted the flu. But it was a light case that she recovered from quickly. Estanislao now became aware that he had not paid much attention to the deaths of Mansos at the Mission previously. He had been too involved in his reading to notice how many had died.

That Spring with the birth of new calfs and the planting of the crops, Estanislao and Narciso were very busy. Each year there were more animals and larger fields, but not enough Mansos to do the work. The Mexican settlers were asked to help more. That meant they kept more of the profits. The Padres were frustrated that there were not more Mansos at the Missions. Padre Duran, especially, was anxious to get as many military expeditions out as possible. The soldiers could recruit new converts quickly. It was faster than waiting for a few starving Indians to come in on their own.

In the Fall of 1826, the hides and tallow were collected from the cows. Estanislao was weary of all the waste associated with this process. But he kept the Mansos working at a furious pace, as usual. Some of the sailors from the Spanish ship that bought the hides and tallow, were ill and had to be cared for at the Mission. They had been in Panama for several weeks repairing their ship before coming to the Mission San Jose. The passage around Tierra del Fuego had been especially difficult on the ship this time. Estanislao did not have time to worry about the sick sailors. He was too heavily involved in his work. Estanislaa was, however, very busy helping to care for the sick sailors. There were only 6 of them, but it was her job to care for them, bring them food, water, empty their bed pans and launder their clothing.

One evening, Estanislao came to visit Estanislaa. She was caring for the sick sailors inside the Mission living quarters. As Estanislao approached the living quarters, he saw Padre Duran speaking with the Captain of the ship. Padre Duran had a small chest that he handed to the Captain. As the Captain took the chest, Padre Duran said "My friend, we have known each other since childhood. Our fathers are friends. I know I can trust you with this. This chest will help me with my retirement. It is not much compared to what you earn as a ship's Captain, but it will be enough for me."

These words resonated in Estanislao's head. He quickly hid in the shadows so the Padre and the Captain would not see him. Estanislao suddenly understood what Rafael had said to him long ago. The settlers stole calfs from the Mission. The Padres did not complain about it, even though they controlled the soldiers who could have easily gotten the calfs back. Estanislao had just seen the final piece of the puzzle. Padre Duran allowed the settlers to take the calfs. He received payment for the calfs. The small chest contained the payments, that would now be taken to Spain and put into a bank account for Padre Duran's retirement. Of course, none of these transactions ever appeared on Estanislao's ledgers and could never be traced.

Within two weeks, Mansos started to die by the dozens every day. They developed fevers, coughs, red spots on their faces and necks and died within a few days of the appearance of the spots. The Padres were alarmed. They said the disease was the measles for which there was no cure. All the sailors had survived the measles. The Mansos, however, were much more susceptible to the measles and died quickly. Estanislao had to organize a team of men with horse drawn carts to go through the Manso village every morning and evening to collect dead bodies. Every evening there were mass burials for the dead, all buried in a common grave. The Padres could not keep up with recording the names of the dead. After every evening burial service, Padre Fortuni announced that this was the will of God.

Estanislaa came down with a high fever, but did not have spots. Orencia already had spots on her face. She had worked tirelessly caring for the sick Mansos. Unfortunately, she had never seen the measles before and did not know how to cure it. All she could offer was willow leaves to help with fever, aches and pains. Estanislao did not know what to do in the face of this devastation. All he could do was take Orencio and got out for a morning run, every morning. They ran long and hard. Estanislao prayed for the Mansos while they ran. Within a few days, Orencia was dead from the measles. Somehow, Estanislao and Orencio were not affected. They mourned their mother. There were so many dead that day, Estanislao could not make a separate grave for his own mother.

Estanislaa continued her fever and chills on and off. She would have a day or two of malaise with no fever, followed by a day or two of severe headache, shaking chills and high fever. She told Estanislao that one of the sailors she had cared for had the same disease. Padre Duran had cured him with something called Jesuit's bark. Estanislao was surprised to hear this. He thought all the sailor's had the measles. Estanislaa said "No. There was a seventh sailor, kept in a separate room by himself. He had a disease the Padre called malaria. No one went into his room but me. I even administered the tea made from Jesuit's bark to him."

Estanislao ran to Padre Duran. "My wife has malaria. She has sent me to get Jesuit's bark from you, please Padre." The Padre looked at him and said, "Estanislao, are you a doctor now? How do you know how to diagnose a disease, especially a disease like malaria that does not occur in California?" Estanislao said "Padre, my wife cared for the sick sailor who had malaria. You provided Jesuit's bark for her to administer to the sailor. You cured him of malaria. Now my wife needs Jesuit's bark." The Padre said "Estanislao, I am very sorry to hear your wife is sick, especially after you have already lost your mother. But there is no more Jesuit's bark. I will pray for your wife." He turned and hurried away.

Estanislao was stunned, but what could be done? There was no more medicine. He returned to Estanislaa to tell her there was no more Jesuit's bark. She was in the middle of another paroxysm of shaking chills. He was not sure if she heard him speak to her. That night, Estanislaa's fever subsided. She woke Estanislao and told him to leave their home immediately. "Malaria means bad air. The disease is caused by bad air that I got from the sailor. You will get it from me unless you leave." She pushed him out of the hut. Estanislao spent the night with the bachelors.

The measles continued to ravage the Mission. Every day more Mansos died. Estanislao passed by his home every day and called his wife's name. After a week, she did not answer. He entered the hut to find her body, already stiff with rigor mortis. He let out a scream of agony. He had now lost almost everyone dear to him. That evening at the funeral, the Padre was very sympathetic to Estanislao, but said the familiar phrase "It is the will of God."

Narciso was also devastated by the measles. He survived, but lost his wife and their 3 year old daughter. He had already lost his father and brothers in the Orestimba Creek massacre. All he had left of his family was his mother who lived with the Mokelumne.

The measles epidemic lasted almost two months. The Padres had not bothered to count the dead after the first hundred or so. Estanislao had kept track. There had been nearly 400 dead from measles and one from malaria. Winter was quickly closing in on the Mission. He hoped they would get through the winter without more death. He prayed that God would have blessings for them in the Spring.

Estanislao 4 – Estanislao leaves the Mission

When the Spring of 1827 arrived, Estanislao had seen enough death from Spanish diseases, and seen enough of what the Spanish called the will of God. If he had kept his family away from the Mission, they may all be alive now. Among the Laquisumne, the winters were hard times, but at least if a family worked hard storing acorns and salmon jerky, and were careful, they had a good chance of surviving. The Spanish diseases came quickly, mercilessly and killed many people without reason.

Estanislao began having talks with Narciso. When they were out walking in the wheat fields, he consoled Narciso about the loss of his loved ones. They were both miserable over the loss of their families. Estanislao talked about passages in the Bible that he read during his time of mourning. Narciso enjoyed hearing Estanislao's perspective. He had already heard from the Padres. Estanislao had a different and intriguing way of looking at the scriptures. Estanislao seemed to like scriptures that showed men doing God's will. For instance Moses did God's will by parting the Red Sea and saving the children of Israel. Estanislao reminded Narciso that after all, the Padre's were here to do

God's will and convert the Indians. Narciso said "Yes, and we can do God's will by planting wheat to help the Mission thrive." Estanislao said "Our Mission requires much more than wheat to thrive."

After several such talks, Narciso was bored of talks and frustrated that nothing was being done for the Mansos. He was concerned that there would not be enough Mansos to help plant and harvest the crops. He was angry that the only solution the Padres could find was to send out more military expeditions to abduct Yokuts children. "Estanislao, what our people need is for the Padres to give us the Mission and let us run it for ourselves. After all, that is what they have trained us to do." Estanislao said "The Padres have no intention to ever give us the Mission. Just look at what has happened to the Chumash people. They were promised the Mission Santa Barbara would be given to them in 30 years. When the 30 years were up, the Padres did not keep their promise. Instead, it appears that Mexican settlers are now being given large tracts of Mission land." Estanislao had noticed that the San Jose settlers had changed substantially in the last 5 years. As the older Spanish settlers retired back to Spain, they were replaced by more aggressive Mexican settlers. Narciso said "Do you think the Padres intend to give the Mission to the Mexicans?" Estanislao did not know. He said "They will do whatever profits the will of God. We have already seen several large land grants given to Mexicans near the Mission. After all, God has blessings for people who help themselves."

The next day as they walked, Narciso said "Estanislao, you are much more clever than me. What do you think we should do?" Estanislao said "The only thing that makes any sense is to leave the Mission. The Padres cannot run the Mission without us." Narciso said "All they have to do is invite the Mexican settlers to run the Mission after we leave." Estanislao said "That is true. Then what we must do is encourage the Padres to go back to Spain and leave the Mission to us."

Over the next few days, Estanislao and Narciso formed a plot to encourage defection from the Mission by the Mansos. After this, raids would be launched against the Mission. The raids would encourage the Padres to leave the Mission. Of course, the raids would have to be carefully done in order to avoid loss of life. The raids would be designed to destroy property and frustrate the Padres. If necessary raids would be initiated against the Mexican settlers to keep them away from the Mission. Estanislao would be the mastermind of the raids. Narciso would stay in the Mission as a spy to feed information to Estanislao.

The two alcaldes met with the Mansos in groups of 20 or so to discuss their plot. They did not want to have a mass meeting to alarm the Padres. Estanislao was very persuasive. "We have seen the will of God. The Spanish brought us measles that killed 400 of us. If this is the will of God with the Spanish, we need a new will of God without the Spanish. We need to learn that God has blessings for people who help themselves." Within two weeks, they had the basis for a small army of Mansos to leave the Mission and participate in night time raids against the Mission. They counted about 100 men who could help with the raids. Their wives and families would help support them by preparing food for them. Altogether, there were about 400 Mansos prepared to leave the Mission.

On May 16, 1827 Padre Duran awoke to the disturbing news that during the night 400 Mansos had left the Mission. They had packed up everything they had and left without warning. He did the quick math in his head, 400 dead from the measles, 400 deserters, this left him with fewer than 1,200 Mansos to run the Mission. This was a crisis he could not endure. He was still Padre Presidente of the Mission system. It would not look good to his superiors. Besides, it would be difficult to shear the sheep and harvest the crops with so few Mansos. He sat down and wrote a letter to Lieutenant Ignacio Martinez, the commandante of the Mexican Army in San Francisco. The letter pleaded with Martinez to go after the Mansos and bring them back using whatever force was necessary. He also warned Martinez that he had heard about foreign trappers in the San Joaquin Valley. He feared that the foreigners were there to cause trouble and incite the Mansos to leave the Missions. What else could explain why the peaceful and docile Mansos had suddenly decided to leave the Mission. Surely the untrustworthy foreigners would try to prevent

Martinez from bringing back the Mansos.

   The foreigners he referred to were Americans lead by Jedediah Strong Smith. Smith and his company of 11 men had crossed the desert from Utah and had been the first Americans to reach California by land. He was 28 years old, but a skilled and experienced trapper and explorer. He was the first American to cross the Great Basin and the first American to cross the Sierra Nevada Mountains. He and his men presented themselves at the Mission San Gabriel in 1826. The Mexican authorities were outraged. He had entered California in violation of treaty agreements. Governor Jose Maria Echeandia ordered Smith to turn around and leave California the same way he had come.

   Jedediah Smith was not going to come all the way to California and leave without some beaver pelts. He was a trapper. That was how he and his men made their living. Instead of going back across the Mohave Desert, he turned north into the San Joaquin Valley. Fortunately, he ignored the mountains near the Mission San Gabriel. He figured there were too few beaver there. He spent several months trapping beaver, mink, otter, musk rat and hunting among the southern Yokuts people in the San Joaquin Valley. He found several Indians who spoke Spanish. They were renegade Mansos who had fled from various Missions to avoid the cruelty of the Padres and the soldiers. Smith used these Indians as guides, interpreters and learned the Yokuts language from them. Smith was always careful to bring some tule elk or deer meat with him when he visited a Yokuts village. In exchange, the Yokuts showed him where the beaver could be found. The Yokuts thought there were plenty of beaver for everyone. Unfortunately, the Yokuts had no way of knowing how efficient Smith and his men were at trapping beaver.

Smith found several thousand Yokuts people living in the Southern San Joaquin Valley. They lived mostly around the huge, shallow lakes, called Tulare and Buena Vista by the Spanish. They lived largely by fishing and hunting among the enormous flocks of birds that lived at the lakes. Smith had never seen such huge flocks of birds anywhere else. When they took to the sky, they blocked the sun for several minutes. However, there were also many Yokuts who lived along the rivers that flowed from the Sierra Nevada Mountains. Smith noticed that as he moved north in the San Joaquin Valley, there were more beaver, but fewer Yokuts. He wrote in his diary that he had been told most of the northern Yokuts now lived at the Missions San Jose and Santa Clara. He spent several months in the San Joaquin River delta trapping beavers.

By May of 1827, Smith and his men had collected 1,500 pounds of pelts from over 2,000 beavers. He was ready to go back to Utah to the Cache Valley rendez-vous. Unfortunately, the snow in the Sierra Nevada Mountains was too deep. He and his men had to turn back and return to the valley. They made their headquarters along a river he called the Appelaminy. This was where the Apelumne and Laquisumne people lived. There were few of these people left anymore. Smith and his men quickly erected an American style log fort to hold off the Mexicans if they had to.

Estanislao lead his party of 400 to the Laquisumne area. The area was now deserted. No one wanted to live there after the Spanish atrocities occurred. About 100 of the deserters decided to go back to their own people, rather than staying with Estanislao. He encouraged them to go. They could be emissaries to help recruit a resistance to the Mexicans. The deserters set about making huts and collecting food. The men went out duck hunting and fishing. Within a few days, they encountered Jedediah Smith and his men. The fort Smith had constructed was familiar to Estanislao. He had seen drawings of forts in books on military tactics. Smith and some of his men were the first white men Estanislao had ever met who were very willing to speak Yokuts with him. The Padres could understand a little Yokuts, but were always quick to let the Mansos know that Yokuts was an inferior language. Estanislao was also surprised that the Americans were so tall. Most of them were nearly 6 feet tall. This was much taller than the short Spanish and Mexicans, who were mostly 5 feet 4 inches tall or so.

In the meantime, Commandante Martinez had organized his military campaign. He and his men sailed from San Francisco to San Jose. They were now on the march, looking for Mansos to return to the Mission San Jose. Martinez was an arrogant and clumsy military man. He assumed, as all Spanish and Mexicans did, that the Indians were ignorant and would not resist them. Narciso, who had been left as a spy at the Mission, ran to Estanislao to tell him about Martinez. This was completely unnecessary, because Martinez had no intention to go more than a few miles from the Mission. Neither he nor his men had been paid by the Mexican government in over one month. The government decided that it was too expensive for them to pay the soldiers, who were after all being cared for by the Missions. The soldiers were very angry about this and did not know how they would ever retire to Spain or Mexico with no pay. This lack of pay took away their interest in fighting Indians. Narciso had convinced Padre Fortuni that he could find the deserters and persuade them to return to the Mission. The Padre allowed Narciso to leave on this errand. Estanislao sent four men back with Narciso to the Mission to relay information to him. Unfortunately, Narciso and the four others were caught by Martinez as they returned to the Mission. Martinez had put the Mission under martial law. No one was allowed to leave or enter the Mission. When Narciso and the others entered the Mission, they were easily caught.

Martinez was brutal to the five Mansos. On May 26 and 27 he had them beaten to get confessions from them. One of the men died from the beating. Another became unconscious and could not be revived for several hours. Narciso held out as long as he could but realized that if he did not talk, Martinez would beat him until he died. Narciso finally told Martinez that several of the deserters had gathered together to lay claim to the San Joaquin Valley. He told them the deserters had formed an army of several hundred men. He said the land from the San Joaquin River to the Sierra Nevada Mountains to the Columbia River was under their control. In addition, the land facing the river and all the land below was theirs. The Mexicans laughed at this claim. This would put the Mexican border in California just 50 miles from the Mission San Jose. This audacious claim could have only come from the Americans. Surely, no Manso had ever heard of the Columbia River. When questioned about the foreigners, Narciso told them that there were several Americans in the area and that Pacomio, the Chumash leader, was with them. Narciso said the Americans were there to trap and hunt, nothing more.

Among the Mexicans was Capitan Luis Antonio Arguello. He had been the leader of the Mexican Army sent to put down Pacomio's revolt. Arguello bristled at the sound of Pacomio's name. He longed to catch Pacomio and bring him in for a hanging.

In the meantime, reports came in that several Mansos had gone missing from the Missions Santa Clara, San Juan Bautista and Santa Cruz. Martinez began to see that this was a well organized rebellion. Four Missions were involved and more than 600 Mansos. As Martinez considered his options, the Mansos made their way to Estanislao's encampment. The Indian Army grew to nearly 500.

Arguello could not wait for Martinez to act. Arguello sent out Sargeant Francisco Soto and about 20 men to find out what influence the foreigners were having on the deserters and to bring back as many runaways as possible. Soto had no trouble finding Estanislao's encampment. However, the sight of 500 Indians frightened Soto. He did not threaten them or look for Pacomio. Instead he went to visit the Americans. There he found several Americans minding their own business. They were not in contact with the runaways as far as he could tell. The Americans were simply waiting for Jedediah Smith to return. He had taken three men with him, the 1,500 pounds of pelts and had headed across the Sierras to the rendez-vous in Utah. The snow had melted somewhat allowing them to cross the huge mountains.

Soto found Abraham Laplant among the Americans waiting for Smith. Laplant spoke Spanish, as well as French and many Indian languages. Laplant produced letters written by Jedediah Smith to Padre Duran, the last one dated May 19, 1827. The letters told Duran that Smith was doing everything he could to leave California, but was hindered by snow in the mountains. Smith's second in command, Harrison G. Rogers, sat down and wrote a letter to Capitan Arguello. The letter pleaded with the Mexican to allow the Americans to stay in California for a few more months until Smith returned from Utah.

Sargeant Soto returned to the Mission San Jose with his timid report that he had found the runaways and thought they were not a threat to the Mexican Army. He had also found the Americans and was not afraid of them. After hearing the size of the Indian Army, Arguello decided to accept Soto's report and recommendation that the Indians were not a threat. His report to Governor Echeandia on June 6 stated that the "the Americans, shameful and cowardly though they were, had apparently not caused an insurrection among the Christian Indians."

The actual fact was that the Americans were doing everything they could to help Estanislao. Abraham Laplant was sent to talk to Estanislao. He had learned Yokuts quickly and could carry on a fair conversation, with only the occasional need to add a Spanish word. Abraham said "My mother was an Indian. My father was white. My mother came from the Cherokee people. They used to live in the United States in a place called Tennessee. My father was French, but had become an American. He was a long knife, one of the white men hired by the US Army to fight Indians. They were called long knifes because they carried long Bowie knifes. He fought the Iroquois and Shawnee, who were enemies of the Cherokee and the Americans. The reason for killing Iroquois was to open up the land of Kentucky, Indiana and Ohio for white settlers. He even fought Tecumseh the great Shawnee Chief in 1811. After he had fought the Shawnee and Iroquois for many years allowing the settlers to move into Indiana, the Cherokee nation turned against him and my mother. Many full blooded Cherokees did not approve of a white man marrying one of their women. My father died defending his family. My mother died helping me escape from her own people. I was only 7 years old at the time. I was raised by my Cherokee uncle and aunt in the woods, far away from the hostile people."

Estanislao was not shocked to hear that the US Army were just as bad as the Spanish and Mexicans to Indians. He was very surprised to hear about the full blooded Cherokees turning against the half bloods. He asked "What difference is there between a man who is full blooded Cherokee and one who is half blooded?" Laplant said "The half bloods were more open to changes brought by the white men. The full bloods wanted to live only in the old ways. I thought the full bloods were a bunch of liars. Many of them lived in white man style houses with large farms and orchards. They lived just like white men. Some of them even had black slaves. They liked to talk about the sacred and balanced way of life that God wanted them to live. I could not see anything sacred when they killed my mother." Laplant told Estanislao that Smith and his men would do everything the 12 of them could to help.

The next day, Estanislao accompanied
Laplant on his beaver trapping outing. They went
out early in the morning and walked up the bank
of a large stream with many willow trees on both
banks. Eventually, Laplant saw a small stick
floating in the stream, but not moving with the
current. He walked into the stream and pulled on
the stick. Up came a chain and a dead beaver.
Laplant removed the beaver from the trap that held
its foot. He put the trap on the bank, smeared
some beaver scent on it, and spread it open.
The beaver scent came from the scent gland of
another beaver. He explained to Estanislao that
the beavers came to the willow trees in the evening
and early morning. When they smelled the scent
of another beaver, they always investigated. This
usually ended up with the beaver stepping in the
trap. The first thing any beaver did upon sensing
danger was to jump in the stream. The heavy
trap that was tied by a chain to a tree, eventually
caused the beaver to drown. The stick tied to the
trap helped the trapper to find his beaver. They
continued to make the rounds of Laplant's traps.
He had trapped a dozen beavers during the night.
Estanislao was impressed with the efficiency of
the traps. Yokuts techniques involved shooting the
beaver with an arrow. The pelts were made into
warm winter robes, similar to the Chumash sea
otter robes.

Estanislao recruited Smith's men to help
train his men to make a fort. Estanislao and
several Indians had made some night time visits

to the Missions San Jose and Santa Clara. This involved walking for three days to get to the Mission, waiting until night fall and taking whatever they wanted. The Mansos at the Mission helped them. Then they ran back to Laquisumne during the next 2 to 4 days, covering more than 20 miles each day. The slow Mexicans on their horses could not catch them. They had stolen saws to cut down trees. They had also stolen several horses. It was better to steal horses than cows. Horses were quieter than the noisy cows. They could also run all night long. A cow could barely walk a few miles. They had to run about 60 miles from San Jose and nearly 80 miles from Santa Clara. Horse meat also tasted better than beef.

Unfortunately, the pine trees to build the fort were about a one day run away from the river. Laplant taught Estanislao to use large, regular shaped trees that would form a solid wall with no holes. In addition, they constructed a false wall on the front of the fort. The false wall was made of small, sharply pointed logs. The top of the false wall was movable and could be pushed away from the fort to form a 45 degree angle with the real wall. Any horse rider that encountered this obstacle would be impaled. Estanislao also insisted on digging several basement chambers and escape tunnels. There were escape tunnels leading in all four directions, providing easy escape for the women and children if necessary.

Several Indians came to join the fort building and help create an army to defeat the

Mexicans. Among the first was Pacomio, the Chumash who had lead a revolt against the Padres. Pacomio was a tall, strong man, who was a very likable person, but knew nothing about military tactics. Pacomio brought several Chumash people with him.

Then came Cipriano from the Mission Santa Clara. Estanislao recognized him immediately. His Yokuts name was Huhuyut. He was from the Hoyumne people, who lived not far downstream from the Laquisumne. Cipriano was 38 years old and had married a Laquisumne girl, called Cipriana by the Padres, who had been a friend of Estanislaa. Unfortunately, Cipriana had died in child birth in 1822. Cipriano had remarried in 1824 to Ana Maria, a Yokuts woman.

Cipriano was a natural leader. He was tall, strong and smart. Like Estanislao, he had spent much of his time studying the Mexican soldiers and learning about military tactics. The other Mansos regarded Cipriano as a leader. He had brought nearly 100 Mansos with him from the Mission Santa Clara.

The first fort was large enough to hold 200 people during a battle. They then set about making an even larger fort, up river a mile away. The larger fort was the same design as the first fort. When finished in the spring of 1828, it could hold about 400 people.

The problem of cannons and rifles would have to be overcome. Estanislao had stolen a few rifles and some ammunition. It would not be enough to fight the Mexicans. He had no cannons. Many of the Indians did not want to use rifles. They said it was not the Indian way. However, he remembered the words of Pepe that stronger arrows could penetrate leather armor. He addressed the Indians and asked them to find a strong and straight wood to make arrows. Within a few days, they settled on gooseberry wood. One species of gooseberry had shoots that were very straight. Arrows made from this wood penetrated leather. Willow wood could be used also. It was not as strong as gooseberry however. The people set about making arrows and soon had thousands of arrows ready to go. Bows also had to be improved. The short Yokuts bows were replaced with long bows, similar to the ones Estanislao had read about. The English made long bows that shot arrows that could penetrate even iron armor.

As they finished with the preparations of bows and arrows, the salmon started to run in the river. The salmon turned the entire river red, with their bright red heads. There were thousands of salmon swimming up stream at any moment. It was crucial for the Indians to gather enough salmon to get through the winter. Some of the men chose to spear the salmon with long, barbed spears. They could easily impale one or two salmon at a time and throw them onto the bank for others to collect. Other Indians created small ponds beside the river. They diverted as many salmon as possible into the ponds and clubbed them. The salmon fillets were prepared and clipped between alder sticks with three branches. The sticks were leaned over an alder fire forming a tee pee of salmon fillets. As the fillets cooked, they were smoked as well. Most of the meat was cooked until it made a dry jerky. This process of preparing salmon jerky continued for many days. As the salmon run came to an end, some of the meat was cooked until just done and was eaten that evening during the salmon feast, a traditional Yokuts thanksgiving. God promised the people that if they lived properly, the salmon would return every year. The Yokuts were very careful to thank God for the gift of salmon, and the salmon for their sacrifice. This involved prayers, singing and dancing late into the night.

As Estanislao ate his salmon, he realized that he needed new tactics to defeat the Mexicans. He had new bows and arrows, but would need some new war tactics to use against his enemies. Later that fall, the people gathered for an antelope hunt. This was a simple activity. A group of about 30 antelope were located in an area where they ate carrizo cane. Men, women and older children were sent out to form a large circle around the antelope. Then everyone began to slowly make the circle smaller. They walked with their arms stretched out to their sides. The antelope did not realize that they could easily run and jump through the circle of people. Instead, the antelope ran into the center of the circle. Eventually, men were sent into the center to kill the antelope. The people sang the antelope song to thank God for the antelope, and to show the proper respect to the spirits of the antelope. As Estanislao stood in the circle, he realized that this sort of trickery could be used in warfare. The forts would not be enough. He would devise clever ways to defeat the Mexicans without endangering his own people.

Jedediah Smith knew the Mexicans were angry with him for staying in California so long. But he did not want to leave. There were still plenty of beaver to trap. Beaver trappers had already exterminated beaver from most of the United States. California, Oregon Territory and Canada were the only spots where beaver could still be found. Unfortunately, while at the Cache Valley rendez-vous, several trappers had figured out that Smith had found plenty of beavers in California. The Hudson Bay Company was preparing to send its trappers to California. Smith had to buy time for his men to trap more beavers. He did this by turning himself in to Padre Duran at the Mission San Jose. On September 23, 1827, Smith walked to San Jose, went to Padre Duran and Padre Jose Viader and surrendered to them. Duran was only too happy to take Smith as prisoner. He quickly locked him in the Mission jail. He wrote a letter to Governor Echeandia and another to Commandante Martinez bragging about how he had the dangerous criminal, Jedediah Smith, in custody. He asked the Governor for instructions concerning what to do with Smith. He kept Smith in jail until December 30, 1827.

On Christmas day, 1827 Duran finally brought his case against Smith. Lieutenant

Martinez presided as the military judge. Narciso was summoned as the accuser. Narciso had been the one who reported, after a flogging, that Smith had been in contact with Pacomio. Narciso had suffered considerably from the flogging. It took several weeks for him to recover. He had lost nearly 20 pounds, most of it muscle, while recovering. Narciso had been in daily contact with Smith at the Mission. He was extremely careful to make sure the Padres did not discover these meetings. He had four guards that watched every approach and signaled him with a whistle at the approach of a Padre or soldier. Smith spoke enough Yokuts to communicate effectively with Narciso, in a way the Padres could not understand. Smith made Narciso aware of all of Estanislao's plans. Narciso passed the word along to the other Mansos, who in turn passed the word along to other Missions. By Christmas, the Mansos in most northern Missions knew all about Estanislao's plans.

Narciso made a weak effort to do what Padre Duran expected. He accused Smith of collaborating with the run away Indians and with Pacomio. All his accusations were true, but he offered no proof. Smith denied all allegations. Duran desperately wanted Smith to be punished, at least whipped. He firmly believed that the Mansos had been persuaded to desert by Smith and his men. Martinez was not interested in punishing the American. He found that the American had stayed too long in Mexican territory, but had not encouraged the Mansos to revolt. Padre Duran was tired of having Smith in the Mission. He wanted to get rid of the American and his party of trappers. Since the desertion of 400 Mansos, nothing threatening had happened. An old saw and some horses went missing. But the Padre was not worried about these minor losses. Martinez ordered the release of Smith, and punished Narciso for lying by flogging him. Smith felt very sorry for Narciso.

Smith walked back to his fort near Laquisimas and rejoined his men. He was in no hurry to leave Mexican territory. It was a cold January with unrelenting rain. As the Spring arrived and the beavers emerged from their dens, the Americans started trapping again. They worked their way north and by the summer were into Oregon Territory. Smith and his men did not return to California.

During the Spring of 1828, several Mansos from the Mission Santa Cruz came to Estanislao's forts. They told him about the conditions in Santa Cruz. The Padres there encouraged the Mexican settlers to take cows from the Mission herds. The Mexicans lived in a settlement called Branciforte, near the Mission. As many as one quarter of the herds were taken by the settlers every year. This left few for the Mission to sell. The Mission was very badly in need of money. They did not have enough money to buy saws and tools to help reconstruct the parts of the Mission that had crumbled during a recent earthquake. During the last visit of a Spanish ship to the Mission Santa Cruz, pirates had boarded the ship and had stolen all the money that was to be paid for Mission hides and tallow. The Padres had blamed this on the French pirate Hyppolite de Bouchard. But Bouchard had not been in California for over 10 years. Estanislao had heard of Bouchard. He had burned Monterey in 1818. One of the Mansos, called Diego, had seen some of the settlers giving money to the Padres at the Mission Santa Cruz. Diego believed the settlers, who were the real pirates, paid the Padres for the cows and money they took. The Padres then put the money into their own bank accounts in Spain. Estanislao had experience with this sort of thievery at the Mission San Jose. Apparently, things were much worse at the Mission Santa Cruz.

Estanislao decided on a bold action. He called his elders together that evening. "Men, the Mission Santa Cruz is plagued by evil Padres and evil Mexicans. They steal from the Indians and leave the Indians to die of starvation." He had Diego tell his story. The men were very moved by Diego's story of the injustices at the Mission. Estanislao then said "Who will go with me to Santa Cruz to teach them a lesson? Who will go with me to help the Padres decide to leave California and return it to the Indians?" Cipriano was among the first to volunteer. Estanislao's brother Orencio, now 19 years old, also volunteered. After much debate, it was decided that a force of 25 men would go to Santa Cruz, wait until night, and attack the presidio.

They would recruit as many of the Santa Cruz Mansos to help as possible and would do as much damage as possible. They would surprise the Mexican soldiers and leave as quickly as possible to avoid being injured themselves. They would use only bows and arrows, no Spanish weapons.

As they were leaving, Sabulon, Estanislao's older brother, by another mother, came to join them. Estanislao was very happy to see his brother. He learned that Sabulon had been living with the Hoyumne people after Laquisimas was abandoned.

The walk to the Mission Santa Cruz took almost five days. They had to be careful to not be seen by the Mexicans. This meant they had to hide in the bushes whenever they saw Mexicans or Spaniards on the road. The Mission Santa Cruz was a small Mission compared to San Jose or Santa Clara. There were only 500 Indians working there. The herds were scattered and mixed freely with the settler's herds from nearby Branciforte. Estanislao enjoyed the area with the beautiful views of the ocean. The presidio was small and close to the Mission. There were only about 20 soldiers at the presidio. As the night came, Estanislao and his men could hear the soldiers laughing and singing as they got drunk. Around midnight, the soldiers finally quieted down. This is when the flaming arrows were shot into the tule roof of the presidio. The roof quickly caught fire. Arrows were also shot into the tule roof of the Mission on the south wing. Flames quickly shot up. The soldiers were so drunk, they were slow to respond. One of

Estanislao's men went to the Mission and sounded the alarm bell on the patio to warn the soldiers. Finally, the partly dressed soldiers came out of the burning presidio. Some were trying to get their pants on or their boots on as they came out.

Estanislao's men attacked quickly and easily took away all the rifles from the drunken soldiers. The soldiers were quickly roped like cows and tied up in front of the presidio. The rifles were thrown back into the presidio to burn. Several Mansos came out of their homes near the Mission. Cipriano and Diego spoke to them and encouraged them to leave the Mission and join Estanislao. In the meantime, Estanislao entered the burning Mission wing. He wanted to leave a permanent message for the Padres. He used a Mexican sword to carve a very large S in the wall using three strong strokes. This would tell the Padres who had been there.

About 100 Indians left the Mission Santa Cruz that night. Most of them went back to their native ways. But 20 of them went with Estanislao. The Indians who went back to their native village areas would be sought by the Padres and hounded by the Mexicans. The other Indians stayed at the Mission to see if the Padres would eventually give them the Mission. They also made sure the Padres had received the message that Estanislao had done this.

Estanislao and his men each took two horses and began the long run back to their forts. By the next morning, when the Mexican soldiers were sober enough to untie themselves, Estanislao was over 20 miles away. The men covered ground quickly on the run home. They were back at the forts within 3 days. After resting for several hours, they were able to tell their story. The news of their great success was very well received. That evening, they had a celebration to announce their victory to everyone. The celebration involved singing Yokuts songs and dancing traditional dances around the fire. They resolved to have several more raids on other Missions to send the message to all the Padres and soldiers.

During the Spring of 1828 an unexpected visitor came to Estanislao's forts. Chief Te-mi (pronounced Tay-mee) of the Mokelumne people walked boldly into the larger fort. He was escorted by 24 Mokelumne men and 15 other men from northern Yokuts villages. Te-mi was in his ceremonial regalia with a large, black top knot headdress and a feathered dance skirt. The top knot headdress was made of raven and split magpie feathers such that many of the feathers stuck straight up. The other feathers were at a ninety degree angle to them. The bottom of the headdress was decorated with a 12 foot long strand of eagle down tied into dogbane string, that wound around the bottom of the headdress. The skirt was made of eagle down string with eagle feathers dangling from the ends. He was about 6 feet tall, thin and very muscular for a man nearly 60 years old. His escorts were equally tall and muscular.

The Mokelumne lived east and north

of Laquisumne on the Mokelumne river. The Mokelumne had not been decimated by Mission recruitment. They lived too far inland for the Padres to be interested in them. The village of the Mokelumne had about 100 people, some of whom were survivors from Laquisimas following the Spanish atrocities. The village, like all Yokuts villages, had a down river Chief and an upriver Chief. The down river Chief was in charge of fishing, festivals and births. The upriver Chief was in charge of war, hunting and death.

Te-mi walked into the fort and asked who was in charge. He was told that Estanislao was in charge. He learned that Estanislao was Cucunuchi from Laquisimas. He laughed and said that Cucunuchi could not lead, he was not born to be a leader. His father had been a messenger. Cucunuchi had no right to lead. Te-mi ordered the Yokuts people to leave the fort and return to their proper villages. He was not happy that 10 men had recently left the Mokelumne to join the fort.

Estanislao quickly came before Te-mi. He came alone and was very careful to show Te-mi the proper respect that was due to an upriver Chief. Te-mi, in turn, was very disrespectful to Estanislao. He said "This man, Cucunuchi, has not right to lead. His father was a messenger, not a Chief. You must abandon this village forever. The people living here are not living in the proper balance. There is no Chief. There are too many people. Each village should have about 100 people, only. You take too much from the river and from the bird flocks. You eat horses, not elk and deer. You live in a foreign structure that is not the proper Yokuts house. You have bows and arrows that are not proper Yokuts weapons. Many of you dress more like Spaniards than Yokuts. This is a bad place and must be abandoned."

Many of the people listened to Te-mi and were concerned about what he said. It was true that they were not living in the traditional Yokuts ways. Estanislao spoke while Te-mi pretended to ignore him. "We are gathered here to fight the Mexicans, and the Spanish if necessary. We have lived in the Missions. We know their language. We know their ways. We know how to fight them and beat them. We have an army large enough to defeat the entire Mexican Army in California. We have the bows and arrows to defeat them. We must continue to resist the Mexicans and the Padres or there will be no more Indians left in California. We have seen that Indians die at the Missions. There are more deaths than births at all of the Missions in California. The Padres cannot be allowed to continue or eventually, all Indians will die."

Te-mi, still pretending not to hear Estanislao, said. "I have heard some ridiculous words that the Indians in California will die. Only a fool would believe this, a fool who does not understand the will of God. God wants us to live in the traditional Yokuts ways. If we will do this, we will continue as always, just as the wind continues to blow and the river continues to flow, forever.

My village, Yalesimas, has not lost anyone to the Missions. We are safe because we all live as Yokuts and do not forget to live properly. We do not forget that God wants us to live as Yokuts, not as Spanish or Mexicans at the Missions."

Estanislao said "Te-mi forgets that the Mexicans, and the Spanish before them, come to the villages, kill the men and take the children they want. Then they kill the women and the children they do not want. This happened at Orestimba, Laquisimas and many other villages. This will eventually happen to the Mokelumne also, as soon as the Padres need more Mansos for the Missions. This will be the fate of all Indian villages in California. In Laquisimas and Orestimba the people were living in proper balance according to the will of God when the Spanish came and took our children. We must unite as an Indian nation and fight the Padres and the Mexicans. It is our only hope."

Te-mi spoke again. "You are not living in balance as God intends. You bring Spanish guns, horses and swords to Indian people. God intends for Indians to fight with bows and arrows, not guns and swords. The people of Laquisimas were not living in the proper balance. A man tried to lead who had not been born to lead. He died because he was not born to lead. Hear me. There is no such thing as an Indian nation. There are Yokuts people, Chumash people, Ohlone people and other people. God does not want us to unite to form a single Indian nation. That would be out of balance.

We must stay as single villages according to the will of God. If we try to unite in this fort or anywhere else, God will allow us to be destroyed. We will bring this destruction upon ourselves."

Estanislao was taken by surprise by the comments about a man who was not born to lead. Was Te-mi speaking about Estanislao's father? He would have to find out later. He said "We have seen that Indian revolts are very successful against the Padres. Pacomio, who has joined us, lead a revolt that would have been successful if he had more men. Here, now, we have enough men to defeat the Mexicans. We cannot allow this chance to slip through our fingers. We must be ready to fight the Mexicans when they come."

Te-mi was getting impatient and bothered by this talk. "God himself will destroy you. He will bring a flood, a fire, an earthquake or a famine to starve you all to death. Those among you who are Mokelumne, come back to the village with me now." He ordered his men to seek out the Mokelumne people and drag them back to the village if necessary. None of the Mokelumne, who were already with Estanislao, went back with him. They all hid until Te-mi was gone.

Estanislao had expected this attitude from Te-mi and most other Yokuts people. These people had not seen the devastation the Padres brought. They had not seen their men, women and children killed or abducted. Te-mi was also right that Estanislao had no traditional right to lead. He had not been born to lead. Chiefs had to be the sons of

Chiefs. He had been born to be a messenger, like his father.

That night, Estanislao called a council of elders. The purpose of the meeting was to discuss Te-mi's words and assess the damage Te-mi had done. Cipriano was the first to speak. He was from the Mission Santa Clara. "At the Mission Santa Clara we have seen much death. Our people die and few are born. The Spanish bring their diseases to kill us and call it the will of God. They promise us that the Missions will some day be ours. Yet we have seen them break this promise already to the Chumash. The Ohlone people are already nearly gone because of the Missions. We must fight against the Mexicans and drive them back to Mexico. We must force the Spanish to go back to Spain. We must reclaim our land for our people. This is our sacred obligation to our people."

Pacomio spoke next "My friends, thank you for inviting me to live here with you and help you with this important work. I am from the Chumash people. When the Spanish first came to us, many years ago, we wanted to help them and even learn from them. I have learned that contact with the Spanish and Mexicans only leads to the death of my people. The Spanish promised that after 30 years, they would give our land back and they would return to Spain. They lied. Instead, the Mexicans have come and taken all the land. No Chumash people have been given land, only Mexicans. I am here to fight beside you. I am here to get our land back and get rid of the Mexicans and Spanish."

Several other elders spoke. None of them spoke in favor of Te-mi. None wanted to go back to their villages and forget about fighting. Most of them had no villages to go back to anymore.

Te-mi had left the Mokelumne down stream messenger with Estanislao. The down stream messenger was to relay messages of peace to Te-mi. Among the Yokuts and all other California Indians, there were strict taboos against harming messengers. Estanislao asked him "Who did Te-mi refer to when he said a man at Laquisimas had tried to lead who was not born to lead?"

The messenger said "Cucunuchi, the Mokelumne and the Laquisumne were at war many years ago. You were not among the men fighting. The Laquisumne up stream Chief was wounded and lay dying. Your father, Sucais, lead the Laquisumne against Te-mi and would have killed Te-mi. Instead, Te-mi told his men to kill Sucais first."

A Laquisumne man said "I was there. Sucais was only trying to get the up stream Chief out of danger. He was dying anyway. We could all see that. He should have been allowed to die with his own people. Instead, Te-mi and four of his men attacked Sucais. Te-mi had his four men hold Sucais while Te-mi slit his throat."

Estanislao finally knew why his father had died. Previously, he had only heard the Laquisumne version of the story. Te-mi had dishonored his father and the up stream Chief.

Te-mi had killed Sucais when Sucais was not attacking him. This was against the rules of Yokuts warfare. War was conducted to capture slaves and take possession of oak trees and fishing areas. War was not conducted to kill, even though sometimes people died. Te-mi had fought against the Laquisumne to kill. The Laquisumne up stream Chief had been wounded during the battle. Te-mi should have declared peace and should have allowed the Chief to be taken to his village to die. Te-mi was the one out of balance with the Yokuts ways.

Estanislao was furious to hear why his father had died. He took several minutes to compose himself. He thanked the messenger for passing on this news and dismissed him without a message for Te-mi. This was unusual. A down stream messenger was supposed to carry happy news. Returning to the Mokelumne without any message would tell Te-mi that Estanislao was angry.

Estanislao 5. Estanislao prepares his army

Soon afterward, Estanislao and Cipriano planned their next Mission raid. The idea was to harass the soldiers and leave the Mission alone. They would ambush the soldiers on their normal Thursday afternoon outing. The plan was not to kill the soldiers, but to take their horses and weapons, leaving them defenseless. This would surely demonstrate to the Padres how useless the soldiers were at defending the Missions.

The sun had not come up yet. Estanislao was crouched in the tules beside a pond. He wore his top knot headdress made of magpie, raven and snow goose feathers. It was black on top, with a knot of feathers that stood straight up. The bottom was white from the goose feathers. The bottom also had his eagle down string wound around it. The eagle down string was made by twining small, eagle body feathers with dog bane fibers. The eagle down string could only be worn by hunters and warriors. The head dress made him look like a large, unusual bird hiding in the tules. It was his turn to hunt and provide for the people, a job that he thoroughly enjoyed. Eventually, several Canadian geese swam nearby. Estanislao quickly shot an arrow. The arrow skipped across the water surface like a flat stone. The arrow foreshaft had a roll of dry tule around it. This made the arrow skip across the surface of the water. It struck a fat goose in the chest. Estanislao removed his head dress and swam out to get his goose. Within an hour, he had four more geese.

As he was walking upstream to the lower fort, he saw a strange person in the distance. It looked like a person with a very large, hunched back. The person was walking toward him at a fair pace. The person was dressed in skins and had long, black hair like an Indian. Estanislao sat down on a log and waited to see this hunch back.

Soon he could see the person was not a hunch back, but was carrying a large burden basket covered with a skin. He laughed at himself for thinking the person was a hunch back. He realized he had not seen anyone carrying such a large burden basket for several years. As the person approached him, he saw that it was a woman. She had twisted hair, a sign that she was a healer on an outing. However, she was dressed as a Chumash man, with a deer skin shirt and a loin cloth. This meant that she expected to be addressed as a man.

The person spoke to him in Yokuts with a southern accent, perhaps from the Buena Vista Lake area. He said "Hello. I am a healer from Gontop. My name is Gaskakwattay, which means red tailed hawk. I am Chumash. I am looking for Estanislao." Gontop was where the most powerful healers lived. It was the site of the most well known medical school in the area. Gontop was in the mountains just south of Buena Vista Lake, near a place the Spanish called Mount Pinos. Chumash, Yokuts and other people went there to learn to be healers. Estanislao said "I am Estanislao. Welcome to Laquisimas. Have you eaten?" Gaskakwattay said "I have eaten, thank you. I have been walking most of the night and would like to find a place to rest." Estanislao lead the healer to the fort and introduced him to several others. He then showed Gaskakwattay where he could rest, in the men's quarters. The healer said that he would rest, after that he wanted to talk.

Some of the Yokuts men in the fort were taken aback. They asked Estanislao if they needed a woman pretending to be a man in their fort. Estanislao said "We will respect the rights of Gaskakwattay. He dresses as a man. We will treat him like a man. We can use a healer, especially one from Gontop." One of the Yokuts said "If he wants to marry a woman, will we allow that too?" Estanislao said "That is a privilege that Gaskakwattay will have to earn. He will have to prove that he can take care of a wife. This is the normal Yokuts way."

Later that evening, Gaskakwattay was invited to join in the goose feast collected by Estanislao and several others. Estanislao wanted to know why Gaskakwattay was there. In Yokuts and Chumash society, a woman homosexual is not usually a healer, but is usually responsible for caring for the dying and prepares bodies for burial. Estanislao asked "Why have you come here?"

Gaskakwattay said "My family is a bounty family. The Spanish Padres will pay to have our dead bodies delivered to the Mission Santa Barbara. I am here to fight the Spanish and kill them or send them back to Spain." Estanislao asked "How much is the bounty on your head?" Gaskakwattay said "My younger brother was killed for a bounty of 5 pesos. I assume I would bring about the same bounty. My father was killed for a bounty of 15 pesos."

Estanislao had not heard of the Padres putting bounties on Indians before. "Why did the Padres put a bounty on your family?" Gaskakwattay said "My family are all Chumash leaders, healers and religious people. My family all have decided to stay with the traditional Chumash ways and not adopt the Spanish ways. My father and my older brother are both Wotes, which means chief in Chumash. They tried to lead Chumash people away from the Spanish and back to Chumash ways." Estanislao now understood. The Spanish would see the healer's family as dangerous. Still it was shocking that the Padres would be willing to pay so much bounty, considering that their yearly budget given by the Pious Fund was only 400 pesos. Estanislao thought there could actually be some Indians who would be glad to turn in Gaskakwattay for 5 pesos.

Estanislao said "Among the Yokuts, a warrior must be a man who has proven himself through many trials. He must have passed through the Datura trial. He must have shown that he is a good deer hunter, goose hunter and fisherman. He must have made his own bow, arrows and ceremonial regalia. He must be invited by the elders to be a warrior." Gaskakwattay said "I have passed through the Datura trial many times, since I am a healer. I have made my own bow and arrows. I have killed deer, geese and have fished in the ocean. I have ceremonial regalia." Estanislao said "You dress as a man and act as a man. I respect you and treat you like a man. However, you must be a man to be a warrior." Gaskakwattay said "These are changing times when the old traditions must be flexible. The traditions can be flexible like willow, but not break. There are important tasks that must be done. We must rid our land of the Spaniards and Mexicans. I want to defend my land and my family."

Estanislao called his elders together to discuss the request. This was very unusual, a woman, healer who wanted to go to war. The elders discussed most of the night. They ate a lot of tobacco to stay awake. They smudged white sage to send their prayers for guidance to God. Many votes were cast, usually ending in a tie. Most of the older men were against Gaskakwattay. Most of the younger men voted for the healer. In the end as morning approached, it was decided to allow Gaskakwattay a chance to prove that he could run with the warriors. Estanislao said "My brothers, we have prayed for guidance. We have very seriously considered this issue. We have finally come to an agreement. We are all bound by this agreement and must not speak against it."

Gaskakwattay joined the training sessions in preparation for raiding the Missions. The training prepared the warriors for attacking, disarming and tying up the soldiers. The healer proved to be very quick, but not necessarily strong. Gaskakwattay was very disappointed with the instructions to not kill any soldiers. However, all the Indians participating in the raid were required to promise that they would not kill unless it was required to protect their own lives.

Later that week, 50 warriors including Gaskakwattay prepared to go to the Mission Santa Clara to raid the soldiers. The warriors prepared themselves with yucca sandals, bows, arrows and some salmon jerky. They would walk for about 3 days, raid the soldiers and run back in 2 days. They all wore loin cloths and deer skin shirts. Gaskakwattay used a band of deer skin tied around her breasts, under her shirt for support. Estanislao knew that it was a tradition for Yokuts, Chumash and other women to be able to run for long distances.

That night, after eating some preserved deer meat and chia seeds for dinner, Gaskakwattay came to Estanislao. "I have never been in a fight like this before. Tell me what to expect." Estanislao said "It will be easy enough. We just have to make sure we surprise the soldiers, knock them off their horses, quickly tie them up and run away. The only hard part will be in making it quick." Gaskakwattay said "I am concerned that my arms will not be strong enough to pull a man from a horse and tie him up. I have fought with my brothers before, but this is a real fight." Estanislao said "You will work with a Yokuts man as a pair. It will not be that hard." Gaskakwattay had more to say, but could not say what she had in her mind. Estanislao sensed that she was afraid. "There is no reason to be afraid. We will all be together, working in pairs. Everything will be fine." Gaskakwattay said "I have never been in a real fight before. Tell me what to expect." Estanislao said "Everyone is afraid when going into a fight. That is natural. You must be afraid, but not paralyzed by fear. If fear paralyzes you, it will be dangerous for all of us. We need you to do your job. You must be quick and sure. Can you do this?" Gaskakwattay said "I will pray and let you know." The next morning, Gaskakwattay told Estanislao that she was ready to fight.

It was Thursday afternoon, the soldiers were tired from riding all day. They were getting hungry and anxious to be back at the presidio. But they still had another hour or so to ride. There were 24 soldiers out that day. All of a sudden the bushes came alive. The trees started to shake. Before anyone could draw his gun or sword, each soldier found himself on the ground with one or two strong Indians holding him down. However, the Capitan had retreated as he saw the Indians jump out of the bushes. Now, he brandished his whip to teach the Indians a lesson. Estanislao saw the whip come out. He quickly jumped at the whip as it was being drawn back from the first strike. Estanislao grabbed the whip and pulled it out of the hands of the capitan. Estanislao now brandished the whip far more expertly than the Capitan. He used the whip to bring the Capitan down from his horse, by whipping it around his body and pulling him down. Estanislao and Cipriano stood by watching as the Indians quickly tied up each man with rope from his own horse. The hands and feet were tied, just like tying a calf. They took off each soldiers' boots and left them as quickly as they had come, without a word. This is exactly the kind of attack Estanislao knew they were most vulnerable to. The soldiers, in their arrogance, assumed that Indians would not attack.

The Indians lead the horses away at a fast trot. As they left, several of the soldiers swore at them calling them stinking Mansos and other names. The soldiers would eventually untie themselves and enjoy a two hour walk back to the Mission with no boots. When they were a few miles away, the Indians stopped to assess their situation. No shot had been fired. No one had been hurt, except for one fat soldier who hurt his shoulder when he fell to the ground. The Indians had used lances made of yucca stalks or long sticks to push the soldiers off the horses. Then they had jumped on the soldiers and tied them up, quickly and expertly. No Indian had been hurt. They continued their run back to the fort.

After running all night and for a very long day, they entered the fort. Estanislao had allowed each warrior to ride a horse when necessary to rest briefly. Otherwise, they ran. They were cheered by all the Indians as they told their story of success against the soldiers. They celebrated by singing and dancing. Each warrior danced to tell the story of what he done in the raid. Estanislao was surprised to hear Gaskakwattay sing Chumash songs. They were very similar to Yokuts songs. Apparently, there had been much trading of songs among the Chumash and Yokuts people. Estanislao was happy with the results of the first raid. He thought "God has blessings for people who help themselves."

They had brought back the Spanish guns and ammunition. Estanislao wanted to use the guns to show the newer recruits what guns can do, and to show them that the fort would stop bullets. Estanislao and Cipriano were pleased with their first raid. They hoped this would be the first of many such raids. They wished that the raids would drive the Spanish and Mexicans out of California. Estanislao was very pleased that Gaskakwattay had done well on the raid. The healer would be accepted as a warrior.

Word came into the fort that 35 Laquisumne from Mission San Jose had returned home for their annual vacation. Of course, these vacations were primarily to recruit new Mansos for the Mission. They had an escort of 12 soldiers with them. Estanislao was amazed that Padre Duran was continuing the same old strategy even after the revolution that had taken 400 Indians from the Mission. Estanislao, Sabulon, Orencio and several other Laquisumne from the fort went to the Mission vacation party. They quickly and without danger took the weapons away from the soldiers and told them to go back to the Mission. The soldiers were outnumbered considerably and did not want any trouble. Estanislao announced to the vacationers that they were now free. All of them joined the fort.

They planned another raid on the Mission San Jose for the next week. Estanislao knew that the soldiers would be more prepared for them this time. They would have to use some different tactics. This time, they would use traps to surprise the soldiers. It took some time for Estanislao to explain the traps and train the men in how to make them and use them. This raid would require 80 men, several lengths of rope and a long saw.

It was a quiet and cloudy Thursday afternoon. The 30 soldiers were riding quickly to get back to the presidio at the Mission San Jose after training all day. They were tired, but wary. They knew that Indians had attacked at the Mission Santa Clara. They did not want to be humiliated by Indians. Quietly a large log swung on ropes through the air and knocked about half the soldiers off their horses. Immediately, Indians appeared out of the bushes, from the trees and some from underground hiding places. Another log swung through the air and knocked many more soldiers off their horses. The Indians fell on the soldiers. However, Capitan Alejandro had held back, away from the other men. He did this on purpose, just in case of a sneak attack. He quickly reached for his gun and took aim. A big stick swung through the air and knocked the gun out of his hand. A large Indian flew through the air and threw him off his horse onto the ground. He recognized Estanislao immediately. Estanislao had him tied up quickly and left him to sputter his insults. "Estanislao, you filthy Manso. Untie me or I will kill you." Cipriano, still holding his stick laughed. "I guess the Capitan can kill with words." Estanislao looked down at the Capitan "I am no longer a Manso. I am a free Yokuts. Do not come to Yokuts country or you will be killed." As a parting gesture, Estanislao had the Indians remove the boots and cut the pants from all the soldiers.

The Indians took the horses and ran off into the hills. Estanislao had chosen the spot for the ambush carefully. He knew the soldiers liked to ride a trail through the area. He knew there were large trees. They could tie large logs between the trees and use them to knock the soldiers off their horses. As before, they ran all night. In the morning, they decided to continue running and found themselves back at the fort the next evening. The story of the raid was told. Everyone was pleased that no soldier or Indian had been hurt. Everyone roared with laughter at the thought of the soldiers walking back to the Mission San Jose with no boots or pants.

Estanislao knew that the Padres would now realize how ineffective the soldiers were at protecting them. He had his brother, Orencio, run back to the Mission San Jose and find out how the

Padres were responding to the attack. Orencio was instructed to tell the Indians at the Mission that if the Padres stayed at the Mission, the Padres' safety could not be guaranteed. He hoped this would frighten the Padres enough to make them return to Spain.

Padre Duran was furious. He knew that Estanislao and Cipriano were behind the attacks on the Missions and the soldiers. However, he was not in fear for his own safety. After all, the attacks had not directly threatened the Missions, except for Santa Cruz. Instead, his main concern was that now it would be impossible to get more Mansos at the Mission. The entire Mission way of life would be in danger.

Duran sat down on November 9, 1828 and wrote a letter to Governor Jose Maria de Echeandia. Echeandia had been Governor of California since 1825. In the letter, he described the attacks by the Indians and explained that the attacks threatened the Mission way of life. He also mentioned names. "Everything depends on capturing dead or alive Estanislao from this Mission and Cipriano from the Mission Santa Clara. They have lead the attacks. They steal horses and guns. They attack and strip bare the unwary. They seduce good Christian Mansos away from the Mission." The Padre did not have much confidence that Echeandia would do anything helpful. The Governor was actually partly to blame for this situation. Echeandia had gone around the Missions and had told the Mansos that he would reduce the abuses of the Padres. He even freed some Mansos from a Mission in 1826. Padre Duran interpreted this to mean that Echeandia wanted to take control of the Missions away from the Padres. Surely Echeandia knew that the Missions, especially Mission San Jose, were a potential source of wealth.

Estanislao and Cipriano heard about Duran's letter from their spies later that month. They demonstrated their contempt of Duran's motives by issuing their own statement. "We declare ourselves in rebellion against the Mexicans and the Mission system. We have no fear of the soldiers, because they are few, young and do not shoot well. We claim the interior of California for Indian people. All the land from the San Joaquin River east is ours. All of the land in the San Joaquin Valley to the Columbia River is ours. This will be a new Indian Nation. No Mexican or Spaniard shall come here." When Padre Duran heard of this declaration, he was convinced the American Jedediah Smith had told Estanislao what to say. How else could Estanislao have known about the Columbia River, in Oregon. Of course, Smith was already gone from California. Duran failed to give credit to Estanislao, who had read about the Columbia River in a Spanish book.

Padre Duran was surprised that Echeandia actually approved an attack on the Indians. In early March, 1829 Corporal Francisco Soto lead 20 men on horse back from the Mission San Jose up the Mission Canyon, along the Arroyo Las Positas, over Patterson Pass and into the San Joaquin Valley. They camped at Laguna del Blanco and were only 14 hours march away from Estanislao's fort. However, as they started the next day, they heard a war cry. Several Indians appeared in the woods and called Soto's name, taunting him, calling him a coward. Soto was never a man to control his temper. He was only 5 feet 2 inches tall and always felt inferior since he was short. He called toward the Indians "Defend yourselves and prepare to die." He and his men brandished their guns and dived into the woods after the Indians, even though there were many more Indians than soldiers.

All the soldiers were quickly dragged off their horses and beaten with sticks. The soldiers quickly retreated back out of the woods, except for Soto who continued advancing. His rifle had been taken from him. He drew his sword and thrust futilely around him. The underbrush was thick making his passage difficult. It did not help that he was being pelted with rocks and sticks. He swore at his opponents and called them to face him. They continued pelting him. Eventually, he retreated, bruised, bleeding and having lost most of his pride. As he emerged from the woods, he called to his men to fire at the Indians. The four soldiers who still had guns opened fire. Estanislao and Cipriano agreed that now was the time to test out their arrows. They called for their men to shoot their arrows. A storm of arrows came out of the woods, aimed at the soldiers with guns. All four of them were dropped immediately. Two were dead. The other two were fatally wounded. Soto himself had drawn his pistol and was rewarded with an arrow in his eye, a wound that he would die from later at the Mission San Jose. The improved arrows easily pierced the soldier's leather jackets. The Indians cheered as they saw Soto and his remaining men turn and run away. It would be a long march for them back to the Mission.

It had been their first real military action. They had come out of it victorious, having killed two, wounded three and suffered only two wounds themselves. One Indian had been cut with a sword, but would recover. The other wound was a gunshot wound. The bullet had gone entirely through the flesh of the Indian's arm. He would recover. Estanislao reminded his men to hide themselves better. Of course, with 170 Indian men in the woods, Soto's men had many targets. That made their shooting easier. Estanislao was pleased that their victory had been with Indian technology and Indian war tactics, not Spanish. There was a victory celebration at the fort that night.

Gaskakwattay had participated in the campaign against Soto. She was pleased to now be accepted as a warrior. She was also pleased to be able to help heal the two wounded warriors. While the celebration got underway, she was in the woods collecting plants to use as poultices for the wounds.

Padre Duran was furious that the soldiers had lost the battle. Of course, Soto had tried to make it sound as much like a victory as possible before he died. He had insisted to the Padre that they had killed dozens of Indians. Even Cipriano himself had been wounded. The Padre was only too anxious to believe his lies. The fact remained however, that Soto had not even seen Estanislao's first fort. He had been a day's ride away from the fort when he was attacked. The Padre felt that another campaign against the Indians would suffice to conquer them. This time, the fort must be burned.

Sergeant Jose Antonio Sanchez was sent out with 40 soldiers. This time, they equipped their leather jackets with stiff leather collars as added protection against arrows. He also had a small cannon to help him break down the walls of the fort. Sanchez was very confident of victory against the Indians. He had all the scouting reports from Soto and Mansos who had been to the area. He had the superior technology of the Spanish. He would be much more cautious than Soto. He also felt that God was on his side.

Progress was very slow due to the cannon that was dragged behind the column of soldiers. Soto had needed 2 days to get to the Laguna del Blanco. Sanchez required 4 days. He felt exposed camping beside the lagoon, but was confident the Indians would not dare attack him. He felt the cannon scared them away. It took 2 days for him to haul the cannon through the woods and undergrowth and to get to the fort. He was amazed at how big the fort was. He had not seen similar parapets anywhere, except in books. The fort was impressive, made from big logs. He decided to wait until morning to attack.

The next morning, the soldiers formed a line in front of the fort. There was no resistance even though they could see motion inside the fort. Sanchez ordered the soldiers to shoulder their guns and fire. The bullets proved completely ineffective against the fort. The bullets could not penetrate such big logs. After the Mexicans had fired their rounds, several Indians appeared at the tops of the walls of the fort. They all had rifles. They aimed and shot their rifles. Sanchez and his men were ready for the worst, but none of them were hit. In fact no bullets were fired. Sanchez assumed the Indians had no bullets. The actual fact was that the Indians had decided not to fire bullets. They were using the guns only to frighten their opponents. Shooting bullets was not the Indian way. However, frightening their opponents was certainly the Indian way.

Sanchez ordered his men to fall back. The cannon was brought forward. He ordered it to be loaded and fired. The cannon ball bounced off the fort. The ball was completely ineffective. He ordered the cannon to be fired twice more. Both times, the ball simply bounced off the fort. After the third shot, the cannon failed to fire. Sanchez ordered his men to retreat while he considered his options.

That evening, May 10, 1829, Estanislao came to talk to some of the Mansos who had accompanied Sanchez. He spoke to them from the bushes near Sanchez' camp and encouraged them to come join him. He knew them and did not want them to be hurt. He also wanted to get some information from them. Sanchez heard Estanislao speaking and went to the edge of the clearing. "Estanislao, I call on you to repent and surrender. It is not too late. Your lives can still be spared if you will but surrender." Estanislao was amused by the stupidity of Sanchez. Apparently Sanchez did not know that Estanislao had 170 trained men ready to kill him and his small detachment. Estanislao said, in Spanish, "I am not guilty of anything and do not need to repent. Soto advised me to defend myself. If necessary, I will die here." Sabulon, Estanislao's older brother, appeared out of the thicket and fired a rifle straight at Sanchez. Fortunately, he did not fire a bullet, and had only intended to frighten Sanchez.

Estanislao quickly disappeared into the woods and returned to the fort. He had heard some news from the Mansos that made him angry. Padre Duran had written last November to various Missions in Mexico and requested Mexican settlers. Duran wanted more Mexican settlers because he was afraid the Mission would be in danger of economic ruin with so few Mansos to tend the fields and flocks. Duran had promised the new settlers large land grants around the Mission. Mexican settlers were already arriving at the Missions San Jose, Santa Clara, Santa Cruz, San Francisco and others. The Padres were giving away all the land that had been promised to the Mansos. The Padres had to promise large tracts of land and many cows to the Mexicans to get them to move to California. After all, California was an impoverished, backward place compared to Mexico. No one wanted to live in California.

Estanislao called a meeting of the elders that night to tell them the news. Pacomio upon hearing about the Mexicans said "this is happening at the Mission Santa Barbara too. All the land has already been given to Mexicans. The Padres are only worried about keeping the Mission profitable. The Padres are more concerned with the Mission than the Indians." Many others spoke and agreed that the Padres were no longer concerned with the Indians and converting them to Christianity. Gaskakwattay said "the Christians have come here and taken away our religion, because they say their religion is better than ours. But hasn't God always been here for us? They have taken away our medicine, because they say their medicine is stronger. But how did we survive before Spanish medicine? How is it that our people die in the Missions and cannot give birth? The Padres have no medicine for them, and say it is the will of God when they die. We are all bounty Indians now. We must fight to the end to rid our land of Christians."

Finally Estanislao spoke. "We have been lied to by the Padres. They came here to convert us to their religion. Yet all they really wanted was to use us as slaves and make money from our sweat. The Padres teach us that God has blessings for everyone. Yet, the Missions are no longer places of God. They are money making enterprises for the Padres and their Mexican settlers. We must send Sanchez and his men back to Padre Duran with the message that we have heard enough of the Padre's lies. We will not tolerate the Padre anymore."

The next morning, Sanchez divided his men into six squads with the intent of attacking the fort from six different places to find a weak place. Before he ordered the attack, he approached the fort with an interpreter and called for Estanislao to repent and surrender. Estanislao answered as before that he was not guilty and would not repent. Sanchez retreated and sounded for the attack. Estanislao could see the six squads circling around the fort. One of the squads was down by the river, where some children were bathing and swimming. He ordered ten men to exit the fort by one of the underground exit tunnels and rescue the children.

Corporal Lasaro Pina and his four man squad had gone to the river against Sanchez' orders. They were supposed to follow along the top of the river bank. But they wanted to get some water to drink. They saw some children and thought they could be harvested as slaves. All of a sudden several Indians appeared from nowhere and attacked them. The Indians shot many arrows and fatally wounded two men, Ignacio Pacheco and another. Sanchez heard the commotion and ordered another squad lead by Juan Bojorques to go to the rescue. By the time Bojorques got to the river, the Indians were gone. Bojorques reported to Sanchez that he had been able to rescue

Manuel Pina and Lorenzo Pacheco. Corporal Pina had also escaped by not going down to the river. Sanchez was amazed to see the soldier's shields riddled with arrows. The Indians had new arrows that could penetrate even shields.

Sanchez ordered the retreat. He did not want to risk losing any more men. He was beginning to understand that he was hopelessly outnumbered. He was also starting to comprehend the power of the new arrows. As the soldiers were retreating, Andres Mesa stepped into a trap. He was quickly swung up into the trees by a rope that had been set by bending a large limb down to the ground and securing it into a trap with a tight rope. Mesa hung upside down perhaps 70 feet in the air with his foot secured by a noose. Unfortunately, he had hit his head against a tree trunk on the way up. He was already dead. Still the soldiers would be able to make a great story out of this. They would later recount how Mesa had been taken alive by the Indians. They would recount how Estanislao had summoned many Indians from neighboring villages to watch as they hung Mesa by the foot from a tree, then shot him full of arrows. The story would continue that before Mesa was dead, the Indians burned him. The soldiers loved to tell these lies. It helped to generate anger against Estanislao. Padre Duran needed no encouragement to be angry with Estanislao. This was the second defeat of the soldiers. Surely, the Mission way of life was doomed.

The battles against Soto and Sanchez had

proven one thing to the Indians. They could defeat the Spanish by using Indian technology. Estanislao had taught them how to use Indian tactics to defeat the Spanish. There was a feeling of optimism among the Indians. The warriors walked with more confidence than before. Gaskakwattay was especially pleased. One of her arrows had killed Ignacio Pacheco. She had watched as the arrow penetrated through his leather jacket and went into his heart. She now felt at least partially avenged for her father's death. She also felt like she really was a warrior.

That night as the Indians celebrated their victory, Cipriano got up to speak. He had been quiet for several days, which was not normal for him. "My people, we have won yet another victory over the soldiers. We can all be proud of what we have done. We have all learned how to make better bows, better arrows and how to use better war tactics to defeat the soldiers. Yet, I fear the end of the fighting will not come soon. The Padres have shown us that they are very angry with us. They are angry because they want to take more of our children to run their Missions. They are angry because they know that we can now defeat them and prevent them from taking our children. Their anger has taken away their ability to think properly. I believe that Padre Duran is now plotting how he can send a bigger army against us, with a bigger cannon." Several Indians indicated that they would welcome such a battle.

On May 21, 1829, news came that a large

army of soldiers lead by Ensign Mariano G. Vallejo had left San Jose two days ago to fight Estanislao. The army had a huge cannon and more than one hundred soldiers from Monterey, San Jose and San Francisco. Estanislao knew that such an army would move very slowly. He and Cipriano decided to go have a look at the army. They were joined by several other men on their run to the west. They disguised themselves in Manso clothing to avoid attracting attention. They ran all day and finally found the army, near Patterson Pass. There were 107 soldiers, 20 Mansos, about 200 horses and a 12 foot long cannon. This was the biggest cannon in California and had been dragged from Monterey. Estanislao had read about these cannons. They could shoot through stone walls. He estimated the army would require at least a week to get to the forts. He and Cipriano would have much to think about. They ran back to the forts and were home the next day.

Immediately, a council of elders commenced. Cipriano and Estanislao told everyone about the army, the cannon and the probable consequences of conflict with such a force. Estanislao knew that the first fort would be no match for the cannon. The second fort may withstand the cannon, since bigger logs were used in the walls. In addition, the movable, cantilevered outer wall could be lowered. This would provide a slanted target rather than a flat target. The cannon balls may not be able to penetrate a slanted target. The final analysis by both Cipriano and Estanislao was the same, Indian casualties would be high. They would probably defeat the soldiers, but would lose many lives. Sabulon got up to speak "My brothers, it is time for us to chase the Mexicans off our land. Surely if we defeat this army, even at high cost of lives, the Mexicans will understand that now is the time to go back to Mexico. I will stay here and fight." A cheer went up in support of Sabulon.

Gaskakwattay got up to speak. "My people, it is most important for us to survive. We are the ones who know how to defeat the soldiers. We have defeated them many times already. We have Estanislao and Cipriano to thank for teaching us new ways to use Indian techniques. We don't need to prove again that we can defeat the soldiers. It is most important for us to teach other Indians how to use our techniques and defend themselves from the soldiers. If we stay here and die, we will have accomplished nothing in the long run. Indian people will continue to die. The Missions will continue to infest our land like a plague." There were many murmurs of agreement with these words.

Estanislao and Cipriano maintained their silence through the long debate that followed. Late that night, a vote was taken to see how many wanted to fight and how many wanted to avoid fighting. The vote was in favor of avoiding a fight. It was after all, not the Indian way to take many lives or lose many lives during war. Estanislao and Cipriano had secretly agreed with this point of view. However, the Vallejo juggernaut

was on the way and could not be stopped.
Something would have to be done about Vallejo.

Estanislao 6. Vallejo's War

After voting to avoid war, the discussion turned to how to deal with Vallejo. If he was not confronted and slowed down in some way, he would look for the nearest village to slaughter. After all, he had to return to Monterey with a great victory to brag about. It was decided that 40 warriors would stay behind and mount a defense against Vallejo. They would use fire, traps, decoys and other means to slow down Vallejo's progress. Estanislao, Cipriano, Gaskakwattay and 37 others decided to stay. Estanislao convinced his brothers, Sabulon and Orencio to leave and ensure that the family continued. Many of the 40 warriors who stayed were old men who wanted to be able to serve the Indian people the best way they could. Their wives stayed with them to help make arrows.

The next day, hundreds of men, women and children began to move out of the forts. Most of them went far away from the forts, to teach other Indians the new battle techniques. A few stayed within a day's walk of the forts. They intended to continue the Laquisumne way of life after the battle.

The second fort became an arrow making factory. Gooseberry shafts, obsidian points, sinew and feathers were assembled into arrows by the hundreds. The first fort was prepared for battle with traps, decoys, pits and was left abandoned. The decoys were made from bundles of tule and were shaped to look like men. They were placed around the fort to convince Vallejo the fort was manned.

Gaskakwattay began spending the evenings away from the fort. Estanislao did not see where she went. He was to busy with preparations to follow her. Finally, the fort was ready for Vallejo, who was still two days away. Estanislao followed Gaskakwattay that evening to see where she went. He found her next to a small stream. She was sitting by herself, singing. The song was not familiar to him. The words sounded similar to Chumash but different. He assumed the words were in the secret, ceremonial language that healers used during their special gatherings and ceremonies. The song was soothing. Estanislao sat down where he could not be seen, to listen. She sang for a long time. Then Estanislao saw a man with long Indian hair walk out of the stream. He was completely naked. Gaskakwattay stood up and embraced him. Estanislao knew that he was seeing a spirit sent by God to communicate with Gaskakwattay. He left quickly and went back to the fort. He did not want to anger God by being where he should not be.

The next day, Estanislao went to Gaskakwattay. "I saw you praying and singing last night." Gaskakwattay said "I pray every night. I found a peaceful little stream to pray beside." Estanislao said "I hope I don't make you angry or anger God, but I saw a spirit come to you last night and embrace you." Gaskakwattay was not angry and said "There was no one there but me. What you saw was the word of God coming to me. I have been told that what we are doing is right. God will be with us. He will send his protection to us." Estanislao thanked Gaskakwattay for praying for the fort and thanked her for asking God for protection. He was amazed that she could stay so calm on the eve of war.

Mariano Vallejo was born in 1808 in Monterey, California into a wealthy Mexican family. During his youth, he had frequent contact and in fact instruction from high ranking government officials, including the Governor himself. He entered into military service when he was 15 years old and became immediately entranced with warfare. He had been promoted quickly and regularly, as expected for the son of a wealthy man. Vallejo was very inquisitive and in some ways, almost open minded. He was interested in books on government and social structure. He became openly critical of the Mexican upper class society and the rigid class structure. He was very interested in the American form of government. This would lead in 1831, to his unofficial excommunication from the Church for refusing to turn in banned books in his possession. Vallejo was a very ambitious man who wanted to make a difference with his actions. He was not particularly interested in fighting Estanislao, since his real battle was with the rigid Mexican social structure. However, fighting Estanislao could bring him fame and fortune, which might eventually lead to more influence in society.

On May 28, 1829 Vallejo and his army left camp at Laguna del Blanco and came to the San Joaquin River crossing. The river was raging with spring rain and snow melt from the Sierras. The army had to cross the river, since they had to go to the east to find Estanislao. Vallejo ordered the Mansos to build a tule raft to haul the cannon across the river. While the raft was being built. He ordered two soldiers to cross the river towing a rope behind them. This would give them a rope to use to haul the cannon across. The soldiers entered the raging river on their horses. Unfortunately, they chose a shallow crossing place, with many big rocks in the water. Their horses could not navigate the submerged rocks. Both horses quickly fell and were washed away in the river. Ropes were thrown to the two soldiers to save them from drowning.

All 20 Mansos were busy cutting tule in a nearby lagoon. They brought back huge armfuls of the reeds and stacked them on the ground. Then they tied the tules into bundles with ropes. The bundles were then lashed together to make a flat raft, about 15 feet long on each side and more than three feet thick.

Two soldiers were sent across the river at a deeper place, where the horses could swim. The horses labored valiantly across the current and eventually made it across the river. The soldiers riding the horses had played out their ropes as they crossed. Now there were two ropes stretching across the river. Vallejo sent half of his men across the river. They used the ropes to pull themselves and their horses across. Additional ropes were passed across the river until there were ten ropes in all. Now it was time to haul the cannon across the river. The cannon was placed on the tule raft and secured with ropes. The ten ropes from the other side of the river were tied to the cannon. Ten more ropes from Vallejo's side of the river were tied to the cannon. With 5 men on each rope, on both sides of the river, they began to haul the cannon across.

At first the cannon floated well on the dry tule bundles. Soon the tules began to absorb water and became much heavier. The current dragged against the raft with more force as it progressed into the river. The soldier's arms quickly tired. They quickly looped their ropes around the saddle horns of several horses. This gave them a chance to rest. Vallejo ordered that the horses should haul the cannon across. Unfortunately, the five horses were not strong enough to haul the cannon across. Just when all seemed lost, Te-mi, the Mokelumne war chief, came to help. Te-mi had 40 men with him. They heaved on the ropes and were eventually able to bring the cannon across the river.

Vallejo was astonished to see Yokuts people helping him haul his cannon across the river. The Mansos let him know that Te-mi wanted to see Estanislao dead. Vallejo quickly understood that Te-mi would be a great ally in his war against Estanislao. Vallejo and the remaining men crossed the river. Vallejo spoke to Te-mi through a Manso interpreter. Te-mi told Vallejo that he wanted to help kill Estanislao. Vallejo asked Te-mi why it was so important for Estanislao to die. Te-mi said "Estanislao is evil. He works against the will of God. He leads other Yokuts people against God." Vallejo found out that the animosity Te-mi felt toward Estanislao had begun many years ago. Vallejo agreed to allow Te-mi and his men to accompany him into war.

Their journey was soon blocked by the river of Estanislao. Vallejo was now within a day of the forts. But Vallejo was on the northern bank of the river. The forts were on the southern bank of the river. The Estanislao river was not as deep or as fast as the San Joaquin. It could be crossed much easier. He did not want to risk another tule raft crossing. This time, he ordered his men to fell trees across the river. They found bay trees on each side of the river that were 150 feet tall. They cut these trees down so that they fell across the river. By strapping the trees together with ropes, they fashioned a crude floating bridge. They tied ropes to the cannon from both sides of the river, and hauled it, while on its cart, across the bridge. This was nearly as difficult as using a tule raft.

The next morning, May 29, 1829, Vallejo was woken by shouting. He ran out of his tent to see many of his horses running into the bushes. Estanislao and his men had untied the horses while the night watch slept. Vallejo could see Yokuts men running with the horses. Estanislao and Cipriano laughed as they ran with the horses. It was too easy to outsmart Vallejo, who still was trying to get his pants on. Estanislao was not surprised to see that the Mokelumne and Te-mi had come to the aid of Vallejo. Several soldiers gave chase. Te-mi and his men watched the commotion and did nothing to help. Horses were not Yokuts animals. Horses were out of balance with God's order. Eventually, 14 of the horses were recovered. Fortunately, Vallejo had brought many extra horses. He did not bother counting how many had been lost.

Vallejo eventually came to the first fort. The fort was empty, except for tule decoys that looked like men. But Vallejo did not know this. To him, it looked like there were several Indians in the fort. In fact, Estanislao and his men were hiding in thickets near the fort, ready for an ambush. All of a sudden, the air was full of arrows. Several men were killed, including some Mokelumne. Vallejo would not include these casualties in his report of the war. Vallejo ordered his men to take cover and shoot when ready. He ordered Pina, the artillery man, to fire the cannon. Eventually, his men began shooting their rifles, at the fort. But the arrows had come from a thicket nearby. Estanislao and his men had already left the thicket and were running to the second fort. Vallejo had positioned several sharp shooters on the other bank of the Estanislao river. As Estanislao and his men emerged onto the opposite river bank, the sharp shooters opened fire across the river. Two of the older warriors were killed, of course Vallejo would eventually magnify this number in his report.

Finally Pina fired the cannon. Estanislao's men heard it like thunder echoing through the forest. The balls bounced off the thicker parts of the walls of the fort. However, the thinner parts were splintered by the balls. As the fort was being blasted by the cannon, Vallejo ordered the thickets to be set on fire. The bushes were dry and burned easily. However, there was no one left to burn out. When it was apparent there were no arrows assaulting them, Vallejo ordered Te-mi to attack the fort. Te-mi and his men whooped and charged the broken walls. Once inside, several Mokelumne men fell into pits that had been covered with tule reeds. In the pits were sharp willow sticks. Several men were impaled in the pits and died. Vallejo did not bother counting these dead. Vallejo later wrote that Te-mi and his men inflicted a massive slaughter on Estanislao's men who were still in the fort. However, there were actually only decoys in the fort.

As Vallejo prepared to give chase to Estanislao, the fire turned against him. The fire was now raging nearly one hundred feet high and quickly consumed everything it touched. However, the fire did not come near the fort. Vallejo had to quickly move his army and the precious cannon back to the west. Eventually the army was able to go around the fire. However, several horses had panicked and were lost in the blaze as well as some supply wagons. By now, Estanislao and his men had returned to the first fort to see what had happened. They decided to stay and put up a resistance.

By 3 PM, the cannon had been repositioned. Vallejo had some of his infantry in the river bed. The cavalry was positioned to the right of the fort. The Mansos and Mokelumne were sent to the left of the fort. The arrows from Estanislao's men started to fly again. The Indians were hidden inside trenches in the fort. The trenches were connected to escape tunnels. Vallejo's army could not defeat the Indians. Vallejo became frustrated and ordered Sanchez to take 25 men and advance straight at the fort. He ordered that no shot was to be fired until they reached the first palisade. Sanchez and his men crouched behind their shields and slowly advanced, while being bombarded with arrows.

At ten paces from the fort, several of Estanislao's men ambushed Sanchez. They emerged from tunnels under the fort. Tomas Espinosa took an arrow in the bladder and died later at the Mission. Corporal Jose Maria Villa was shot in the left shoulder. Nicolas Alvizu was shot in the head, but survived. Corporal Salvador Espinosa was shot in the right hip. Sanchez was in a desperate situation. Just then, the fire returned and began to burn everything near the fort. Estanislao's men quickly slipped back into their tunnels. Sanchez ordered his men to jump through the flames and get away from the fort. They followed his orders and survived. Many of them were scorched and had much of their hair burned off.

In the meantime, Vallejo was busy avoiding the fire himself, and trying to save his supplies. Vallejo called a general retreat. His army retreated to the plain about a mile to the right of the fort. As they were retreating, one of the soldiers found the shoes of Ignacio Pacheco, who had died in the May 10 raid lead by Sanchez.

That night, the artillery man, Pina, heard someone walk by his cannon. He thrust his rifle toward the man and found that it was an old Indian man carry chia seeds in a large deer skin bag. The man spoke Spanish to him and told him he meant no harm. It was too late for the Indian. Vallejo came running to the scene. Vallejo ordered the Indian to be strapped to the wheel of the cannon and whipped him until he spoke. The old man finally spoke to Vallejo in Spanish. He had come from an upstream village called Tagualame. He was bringing chia seeds to Estanislao and did not know the fighting had already started.

On the morning of May 30, 1829, Vallejo ordered Te-mi and his people to storm the fort. The Yokuts ran quickly toward the fort. There was no response. They soon learned that the fort was abandoned. Vallejo bravely took 27 men with him and approached the fort himself. In his later report he described the situation. "I, myself, went into the fort with 27 well armed soldiers. We found two buried bodies. In most of the pits and trenches we found blood." He neglected to say that the bodies were from Te-mi's people. Vallejo ordered the fort burned.

Estanislao and his men were gone. Vallejo announced to his men that the coward, Estanislao, and his men had run away. They had apparently been able to slip away along a secondary river channel that was not guarded by Vallejo's men.

Vallejo ordered his army to march upstream and find Estanislao. They marched all day and even for three hours after the sun had gone down. The army stopped in a meadow to spend the night. In the meantime, the scouts had continued ahead and found the second fort, near the village called Tagualame. The scouts returned to Vallejo with the news. Vallejo immediately ordered his army to march to the fort.

On the morning of May 31, 1829, Vallejo stood in a clearing with his telescope examining the fort. He counted 40 men and many women. Vallejo assumed that Estanislao did not know about their presence. He ordered his men to quietly approach the fort. Of course, the army had been so noisy, especially with the carts and the cannon, that Estanislao knew exactly where the army was. The Indians called the alarm that started the battle. The battle raged all day with no progress for Vallejo, only a few wounded soldiers.

The next morning, Vallejo was getting frustrated. He ordered his men to set the forest on fire to the north and south of the fort. He hoped that two fires would force the Indians into the center of the forest to be burned to death. He set some of his men to hacking a wide path out of the forest for the cannon to advance. Several cavalry men guarded the path makers.

Vallejo set to interrogating the captive Indian again. The captive was still lashed to the cannon. He ordered the Indian to tell Estanislao and his men to surrender. Vallejo promised that no harm would come to them if they surrendered. The captive knew this was a lie and spoke to Estanislao's people in Yokuts. He told them that more Mexicans were coming through the brush and that the cannon was on the way. One of Te-mi's men, named Matias, spoke to Vallejo and told him, in Spanish, what the captive had said. The captive was immediately shot. Matias then became the interpreter and told Estanislao to come out and surrender. Someone inside the fort shouted back that they preferred to die. Arrows began to fly out of the fort.

Pina brought up his cannon and fired it at the fort. The cannon ball bounced off the cantilevered wall of the fort. However, the roar of the cannon frightened Te-mi's men and the Mansos so much, they refused to advance. The cannon continued to roar during four hours. Still the fort was intact. Vallejo found that he only had 20 cannon balls left. This was not enough to continue the battle. He would have to retreat. He was extremely disappointed. Now he would not be able to brag about his victory. He incited some of his men to draw their daggers and run into the trenches near the fort, hoping to find someone to fight.

Now the fire turned on Vallejo. He found that he could not advance. In addition,

he was virtually surrounded by a raging inferno.
Vallejo ordered Pina to save the cannon and the
ammunition. Then he ordered a retreat. As they
retreated, the fire sputtered and sparked at them.
Some of the soldiers were sure the sounds were
rifle fire, not the sound of the fire. They shot back
in exasperation. Estanislao and Cipriano, inside
the fort, were amazed at Vallejo's stupidity. He
had arrogantly come to war, hoping that his big
cannon would be enough to win the battle. He had
succeeded only in defeating himself with his own
fire.

Vallejo had to find some way to declare a
victory. He marched his army a couple hours down
stream. Then, he ordered his army to surround the
village called Tagualame. The Indians in the village
were completely peaceful. They had been ordered
by Estanislao not to fight. The village was made
up mostly of the old wives of the men fighting with
Estanislao.

Estanislao and Cipriano knew immediately
what Vallejo intended. They quickly organized two
squads of ten men to go rescue the women. It was
ironic. Estanislao and Cipriano had intended to
give Vallejo a victory. But Vallejo's own stupidity
had defeated him. Now Vallejo turned to an act of
desperation to find any victory he could. Estanislao
ordered the evacuation of the fort. They would
leave it for Vallejo, so he could have his victory.

It was already night. Vallejo decided to wait
until morning to attack the village. During the night,
most of the women were able to escape. Their

husbands came to their aid. The soldiers got little rest that night. They were busy shooting at every movement they heard. In the morning, the village was empty except for three old women who had been wounded by bullets. Vallejo had a different view in his official report. "The Indians tried to escape. Most were killed, except for three old women who were captured. The next day we found three old women dead in the bushes." Two old men had been killed during the night helping their wives escape. After this, Estanislao's men called Vallejo, "Woman Killer."

Vallejo's report filed after the battle indicated that, at this point, he had 11 casualties and two wounded Mansos. However, Pina and several other soldiers put the number of dead and wounded soldiers much higher. Even though he had insufficient supplies and ammunition, Vallejo could not allow himself to retreat further. Vallejo was not satisfied with the battle. He only had three old women captives. He did not have enough to brag about.

On the morning of June 1, 1829, Vallejo ordered Matias and the three old, captured women to lead them into Estanislao's fort. One of the women was called Augustina. She told Vallejo there was no one left at the fort. She told him Estanislao had abandoned the fort, so Vallejo could have it. Vallejo left Pina and a small squad to guard the cannon and supplies. The others went with Vallejo to the fort. As they approached the fort, Vallejo ordered that the three old women should be shot immediately. Then Te-mi's men found an old man hiding. He was a run away from the Mission Santa Clara. Te-mi asked Vallejo's permission to kill him. Vallejo consented. The old man was perforated with 73 Mokelumne arrows before he died. Vallejo had his arrow riddled body hung on an oak tree as a sign to other Indians of the danger involved in fighting Vallejo. As they approached the fort, Matias had served his purpose. A Manso killed Matias and hung him on an oak tree.

The fort was virtually abandoned, except for Estanislao, Gaskakwattay and five old men. Estanislao was mourning over the body of his dear friend Cipriano who had died just at dawn. Cipriano had come back to the fort the night before with the body of his wife, Ana Maria. Apparently, Ana Maria had gone to Tagualame during the night to rescue her aunt. Cipriano had gone along. Ana Maria had shielded her aunt's body with her own body and had taken a bullet in the back. Cipriano became enraged at the sight of his wounded wife. In his rage, he had killed 7 soldiers with his hands and his spear. Unfortunately, his rage had been a fatal mistake. He was shot in the abdomen by the seventh soldier. Cipriano had picked up his dying wife and had carried her to the fort to be cured by Gaskakwattay. It had been too late. Ana Maria had died before getting to the fort. Then, despite Gaskakwattay's best effort, she could not cure the bullet in Cipriano's abdomen.

Estanislao sat mourning his friend and paid little attention to Gaskakwattay. She and the five old men were singing a song he had never heard before. They were dancing a dance he had never seen before. Gaskakwattay wore her ceremonial Chumash regalia, with a feathered skirt, top knot headdress made of magpie feathers, and a deer skin shirt. All of the dancers were painted with dark black pigment and decorated with bright white lines and spots on their faces, arms and legs. Soon ravens began to perch on the upstream wall of the fort. Gaskakwattay continued to sing and dance until she saw Vallejo's men approaching the fort. Then she ordered everyone to hide quickly. They all hid in the escape tunnels. Estanislao was less quick to get out of sight.

Vallejo saw that the front gate of the fort was open. He could see no one inside the fort. He was amazed at how big and well made the fort was. He ordered several of his men to shoot into the interior of the fort. There was no response to the shots. He ordered his men to charge the fort. The soldiers ran into the fort with their rifles ready. They found no one inside. Vallejo stayed outside, peering through a crack in the wall and shouting orders. A soldier poked his rifle into the tunnel where Estanislao was hiding. Estanislao grabbed the gun and pulled the soldier into the tunnel. The Cherokee trapper, Laplant, had given Estanislao a tomohawk. He had told Estanislao that a tomohawk is one of the best weapons for hand to hand combat. Estanislao had learned quickly how to use the tomohawk. The soldier died from a tomohawk chop to the neck. Then

Estanislao noticed the soldiers were standing still.
Overhead, a large golden eagle flew slowly by. His
enormous wings made a shadow when he passed
by. Estanislao remembered that the golden eagle
was his medicine animal.

There were nearly 50 large ravens perched
on the upstream wall of the fort. All at once, they
jumped off the wall. As they descended to the
ground, Estanislao saw them transform into Yokuts
men. One of them was his father, Sucais. The
soldiers were too terrified to run away from this
bewitchment. Estanislao ran to embrace his father.
"Father, I have missed you." Sucais said "I have
missed you, my son. I have been proud of you.
You have found how to use Indian techniques to
defeat the Mexicans. You have done well." All
around them, Yokuts men were fighting the soldiers.
The soldiers were frustrated, because the Yokuts
could not be killed. Estanislao and Sucais joined
the battle. Estanislao killed many soldiers with his
tomohawk.

Then Sucais saw Te-mi enter the fort.
He ran to Te-mi and grabbed his throat with an
unbreakable grasp. "Te-mi, my old friend, you are
out of balance with God's will. You have joined
with the enemies of the Yokuts people." Te-mi
could not respond because he could not breathe.
Sucais turned to Estanislao. "Go now, my son, and
continue your work." Estanislao jumped into an
escape tunnel and was gone. Sucais and the other
Yokuts men started to evaporate, except for Sucais'
right hand that remained clutched around Te-mi's

throat. Several Mokelumne men came to Te-mi's aid. But Sucais' hand could not be dislodged. Just before Te-mi succumbed, Sucais' hand evaporated. Te-mi spoke with a harsh voice for the rest of his life due to his smashed voice box.

Vallejo charged into the fort shouting with joy and declaring his victory over Estanislao. He carefully examined the dead and eventually found Cipriano's body. The Mansos identified his body and the body of Ana Maria. Vallejo was overjoyed. He had defeated Estanislao and had killed Cipriano. This would get him a promotion. Perhaps he would be a general someday. He did not bother to thank Te-mi and the Mokelumne. He dismissed them. They were no longer needed. As they left, he ordered the fort burned.

In the afternoon, while marching back to San Jose, Vallejo and his men found some Yokuts women and children gathering gooseberries in a thicket near the river. They were Suenumne people from upstream, and had not been involved in the fighting. Vallejo had them rounded up. The children were tied to a rope by their thumbs. The women were taken to a nearby meadow for the amusement of the soldiers. The Mansos were not allowed to enjoy this amusement. The Suenumne women were raped repeatedly until the evening when they were killed. Vallejo now had a great victory and the children as a prize for the Missions.

Vallejo started the long journey back to Monterey. He had to cross the rivers again and protect his valuable cannon. A Yokuts man, who had been with Estanislao, saw the army pass by and on the evening of June 2, and set a fire to drive them away from his people. The artilleryman, Pina, had to get out of bed and move his cannon.

When Governor Echeandia received Vallejo's report, he was furious. He had come to California to stop atrocities against Indians, like the atrocity against the Suenumne women and children. On October 23, 1829, he wrote a letter to the Commandante of Monterey. "I understand that on recent expeditions among the wild Indians by the soldiers of your garrison and San Francisco, a harvest of children was secured. Without my knowledge, they were given to your neighbors." Echeandia ordered a halt to the harvesting of children, an order that was ignored by the Padres. He ordered Commandante Ignacio Martinez to conduct a complete investigation of the atrocities committed by Vallejo against the Indians.

Martinez was not anxious to put Vallejo on trial. Vallejo was one of his own officers. If Vallejo had done anything wrong, it would reflect poorly on Martinez. Vallejo had made things worse for himself by bragging about his victory. His lies had been printed in every newspaper in California and had even reached Mexico and Spain. In the end, there was a trial, several months later. The judge found that Vallejo's soldiers had hanged two old Indian men and three old Indian women. A soldier, Joaquin Alvarado, was found guilty of shooting an old woman and sentenced to five more years of service as a soldier at the usual pay. Vallejo was not punished in any way.

Estanislao sat beside the river. Flies hovered in the air around him. It was hot and dry. The old men and their wives were gone. The battle was over. Only Gaskakwattay remained. He and Gaskakwattay had buried Cipriano and his wife, in Yokuts fashion. Estanislao was still recovering from the battle. It had gone much as planned, except for the loss of Cipriano. He had already gone around and counted the dead. Among the Indians there were 14 dead and 10 innocent Suenumne women. Estanislao grieved for these women. The purpose of the battle had been to end this kind of killing by the soldiers. He felt despair over his inability to stop the killing of innocent Indians and the abduction of children. Among the soldiers there had been 30 dead and many more wounded. Estanislao himself had killed 10, most of them with his tomohawk. Among the Mansos and the Mokelumne, there were 10 dead. It had been the largest battle in the history of California as recorded by Mexicans.

Estanislao needed to talk to Gaskakwattay. He said "I was disappointed to see Te-mi helping Vallejo." Gaskakwattay said "Sometimes people, like Te-mi, who think they are doing the right thing, end up doing great evil. It is very difficult to do the right thing, especially for people who resist necessary change and let arrogance rule their lives." Estanislao said "During the battle, ravens came to our aid." Gaskakwattay said "I told you that God had promised to protect us." Estanislao said "Did you see any change in the ravens during the battle." Gaskakwattay was vague "I saw the ravens flap their wings in the soldiers' faces." Estanislao had to tell her what he had seen. "I saw the ravens change into Yokuts men. My father was among them. They helped fight the soldiers. I talked to my father and fought beside him." Gaskakwattay said "I wondered who that was. I saw you embrace someone right before you really started to fight." Estanislao said "I am pleased that God sent my father to help." Gaskakwattay said "God sent protection, that you saw as your father. The warriors and I did a ghost dance to invite this protection. I asked for the protection. It was your belief in God that caused the protection to come in the form of Yokuts warriors. God sent us protection, to keep us alive."

Estanislao asked "Why did he send ravens?" Gaskakwattay said "The raven's eyes are mirrors that force us to look into our own souls and see if we are worthy. When we look into our own souls, there is no hiding the truth." Estanislao said "Were we worthy?" Gaskakwattay said "Of course, otherwise your father would not have come to help you."

By the next day, Sabulon and Orencio returned with several other Laquisumne. They found Estanislao in a state of despair. They tried to cheer him up. After all, he had won the battle. Vallejo had gone away with a hollow victory. Estanislao still retained the land and still could lead his people against the soldiers. After all was carefully considered, it was clear that the victory had gone to Estanislao. He had saved his people the best way he could, the Yokuts way. The ghost dance that Gaskakwattay had taught to five warriors became a topic of discussion. Gaskakwattay said "The ghost dance is only to be used for protection, when protection is absolutely necessary. It was necessary for Estanislao and me to survive. The dance is not to be used by people who do not know what they are doing. I have instructed the five warriors to never teach anyone the dance."

Estanislao slowly began to realize that he had indeed defeated Vallejo. A sense of satisfaction came over him. He went into the charred forest on his own, and got down on his knees to pray. "Thank you Lord for helping my people survive despite all the efforts of the Mexicans. Thank you for helping us to defeat our arrogant enemy even though they had much better technology and should have easily defeated us. Thank you for giving us the humility and perseverance to use your gifts to make better bows and arrows to defend ourselves. Amen."

Messengers were sent out to call everyone to a victory celebration. They went as far away as to the Emigdiano Chumash, down south near Tejon. It was now time to prepare for the celebration. Many of Estanislao's men would return to the area with their families. Deer meat, goose meat, duck meat, fish, berries, yucca hearts and other food would be gathered over the next two weeks. Estanislao also prepared to train any visiting Indians in how to defeat the Mexican soldiers. He especially wanted to teach the Indians how to protect their women and children. A constant subject of conversation was how Indians could defeat their enemies despite the powerful technology their enemies possessed.

Estanislao 7. Gabriel comes

Within a week, there were over 200 people living at the Laquisimas site. Most of them were not originally Laquisumne. They all lived in traditional Yokuts houses and mostly wore traditional clothing. One night Estanislao called the elders together. He said "We have all gathered here to live. We must have a leader and a system of government." He had to use the Spanish word government, which was not present in the Yokuts language. "We must decide how to lead our people. We must decide how to live." There was an immediate suggestion to have a traditional Yokuts village with Estanislao as upstream Chief. Estanislao said "I am not born to be a Chief. I cannot lead a traditional village." A former Manso said, "We should start a village based on a different government, and have Estanislao as our Chief." There was a wide consensus that Estanislao should be Chief. Estanislao had read a book about democracy, where everyone has a vote and elects the leaders. He had discussed these concepts with the American, Laplant. He spent about an hour explaining some of the basics of democracy to the people. The other Indians were interested in the idea of a democracy. Some were very enthusiastic. Others were willing to give it a try. They all agreed to have a democracy, where every elder had a vote. They next elected Estanislao to be their Chief.

Gaskakwattay got up to address the elders. "I am a healer and a warrior. I live among you as a man in the Chumash way. Since you have decided to start a new democracy, I suggest you include women in the voting. Women are more important than men, since they bring children into the world." There was much debate about this issue. After some time, the vote was taken and women were given the right to vote and attend the council of elders. Gaskakwattay was not done. "I would like to have a new start for myself. I would like to continue to be a healer. But I want to be a woman from now on. I have had enough fighting." This raised quite a commotion. Everyone knew Gaskakwattay was a woman. But she had earned the right to be a man and a warrior. The debate raged among those who had known her for some time and felt confused that she wanted to be a woman again. Estanislao had always thought of her as a man and could not imagine her as a woman. The final vote was in favor of allowing Gaskakwattay to be a woman.

The next day, Estanislao went to Gaskakwattay. "We have a new village. We need a religious leader for our village. We need a religion for our village. I would like to have a religion that is open to everyone. A religion where God is accessible to everyone, all the time. In the traditional Yokuts religion, God is accessible to only a few people who are properly trained in how to talk to God." Gaskakwattay said "Yes, it is the same way in the Chumash religion. I am a healer and a religious leader. I have been trained in how to properly respect God, Xoy (pronounced Hoy) in Chumash, and speak to him properly in the ancient language. I am allowed to enter the sacred enclosure during festival times and sing the sacred songs to God and dance the sacred dances. These songs and dances are vital to Chumash life because they promote the proper balance between the people and God. Without these songs and dances, there would be imbalance and the Chumash people would perish." Estanislao said "Among my people, there is the same belief that the balance must be maintained. But we are trying to establish a new way of life for our people. We have a new democracy. We need a new religion to be used in our democracy. Or we could find a new connection with God that would allow all of us to talk to God and not have to speak through a religious leader." Gaskakwattay said "I cannot help you do this. The Chumash religion is very old and must be kept as it always has been or the balance will be lost." It was frustrating to Estanislao that a woman could become a man, then become a woman again, but not be able to be flexible about her religion.

Estanislao said "I went to the Mission San Jose with my mother. She wanted to be with her other son, Orencio, and have our family together again. At first, I did not believe the Padres. But, I became a Catholic. At first, I found the religion unusual. I enjoyed the mass meetings with everyone worshipping God together. As I learned more, I discovered that the Christian God was able to make a woman pregnant. She gave birth to the Son of God, called Jesus. Jesus did many good things and helped many people. Then, He was found guilty of calling Himself the Son of God, or even calling Himself God. He was killed for this. At first, I could not believe that anyone could kill God. Then, I learned to take comfort in the fact that God had made Himself human and had lived like us, then died like us. The Christian God knows what it is to be human and to suffer. That is why I worship Him."

Gaskakwattay said "When I was a teacher at Gontop, the medical school near Tejon, a man was brought to us who said he was God. After talking to him, we discovered that he was crazy. He said he was God so people would fear him and give him whatever he wanted. Maybe this is what Jesus did also." Estanislao was troubled by what she said.

Estanislao found himself becoming troubled about his actions against the Mexicans. He had gone into a rage with his tomohawk and had killed ten Mexicans. He went to Gaskakwattay and asked her if he could be forgiven for his rash actions. She told him that the Mexicans had it coming. They had attacked the fort and brought punishment upon themselves. This did not sit well with Estanislao. The next day he went to Sabulon and said that he would be gone for a few days. Estanislao ran to the

Mission San Jose. He hid in the forest until night fall. Then he carefully went into the Mission without being detected. He went to the chambers of Padre Duran who was very frightened to see him. "Estanislao, have you come to kill me?" Estanislao said "No Padre, I do not come to kill but to ask forgiveness." The Padre was very surprised to hear this. He assumed that Estanislao was possessed of the Devil and had gone on a wild killing rampage. Estanislao talked to the Padre for several hours into the night. He told the Padre he was very sorry for killing the Mexicans and had not intended to kill anyone. The Padre slowly began to understand the purpose of Estanislao's actions. Estanislao was angry with the treatment of the Indians and wanted the Padres to leave and return to Spain. He had ignored this message before, but now came to understand.

Finally, the Padre said to Estanislao "I ask your forgiveness. When your wife died, I did not give her the Jesuit's bark that would have saved her. I was frightened and thought there would not be enough for all of us. So I horded it. Can you forgive me?" Estanislao was grateful to hear the Padre actually admit to doing something wrong. Of course, the Padre had done many things wrong and would continue to sin. But this was his first admission of guilt to Estanislao. Estanislao said "I miss my wife very much. What you did to her was very wrong. What you continue to do to Yokuts children and the Mansos is very wrong. I can forgive you, if you promise to be kind to the Mansos and not kidnap anymore children." The Padre wept. His repentance to Estanislao had been very hard for him to admit.

Estanislao said "Father, forgive me of my sins. I have killed ten soldiers with my own hands." The Padre forgave Estanislao and absolved him of his sins. Estanislao left immediately and ran back to the river. The Padre wrote letters to other Missions and the Governor to let them know that Estanislao had been absolved. In his turn, Padre Duran was able to comply with his promise to not kidnap any more children, especially since Governor Echeandia was watching him carefully to make sure no more abductions occurred. Several months later, October 7, 1829, Governor Echeandia wrote a formal pardon of Estanislao and his followers.

By early July, 1829, many hundred Yokuts and a few Chumash had gathered at the Estanislao River to celebrate the defeat of the Mexicans. Large fires were built on the tops of huge boulders to signal the start of the celebration. The first night, several people brought gifts to give to Estanislao to thank him for defeating the Mexicans. They honored him at the fire and remembered Cipriano. There were three days of celebration. All the men and women wore their top knot headdresses and their feathered skirts. They painted their faces, arms and legs with black, red and white paint. Every evening, there was singing and dancing. The children learned the songs and dances, and ate the good food. Estanislao taught several classes in how to defeat the Mexicans with Yokuts technology and better warfare strategies. When all had celebrated enough and had gone home, Estanislao was left with a feeling of accomplishment. It felt good to look back and be proud of what he had done.

The next morning, Estanislao was on his way to hunt ducks before the sun rose. He saw someone in the river bathing. He did not want to be disrespectful, so he did not approach her closely. She was a pretty woman, bathing naked in the river. Suddenly, he realized, it was Gaskakwattay. He had never seen her as a woman before. He realized that it was the Chumash way to bathe every day before the sun rose. He went away quickly so she would not think he was looking at her.

Estanislao worried about how the village could survive. How could all these people find food? He talked to several people who had been farmers at the Missions and asked them if they would help plant crops for the village. Everyone of them declined. They felt that it was not proper to live like starving desert Indians, such as the Mojave, Cahuilla, Papago and others, who had so little food they had to plant gardens. Yokuts people should not have farms. This decision would effectively limit the size of the village to no more than a couple of hundred people. That was the village size the land could support. Estanislao would not be able to maintain a standing army. He would have to content himself with raids on the Missions. Of course, if a large Mexican Army attacked Estanislao, he was sure he could count on several hundred Indians from other villages to come to his aid.

As the village continued to be built and the way of life was reestablished, the question of religion came up repeatedly. Each time Gaskakwattay refused to be flexible about her religious beliefs. Estanislao called a meeting of the elders, of course including the women, now that the vote had decided to include them. In the entire village of nearly 200, only Gaskakwattay was a religious leader. Estanislao asked for comments on how to conduct religious practices in the village. Several ideas were interesting, each person could practice as they chose, a democratic religion could be practiced, a traditional religion could be practiced. Estanislao did not want to vote on the issue quickly. He decided to allow each person to think about this issue for one week before a vote would be taken. Over the next few days, Gaskakwattay became increasingly unhappy as she heard people talk about making a new religion where everyone could have equal access to God.

One night, Estanislao woke up sweating and shaking. He had been dreaming about heaven, eternal life, what it means to live forever, what it is like to die, and what God is like. These were questions that had bothered Estanislao since he was four years old. When he was about seventeen, these questions had become a source of great anxiety for him. This great anxiety had lasted for over three months. He realized he could not understand the answers to these questions. Still he tried to rationalize the questions and focused on them until he was full of anxiety. The next morning he went to Gaskakwattay and told her about his dreams. Gaskakwattay said "We all have these thoughts and questions. Most of us do not focus on them until we become paralyzed with fear. You need to let the questions go out of your mind as easily as they come into your mind. For most of us, God speaks to us like wind in the leaves. God speaks to you like thunder in the night." These words did not comfort Estanislao. He said "God has cursed me with this burden of speaking so stridently to me."

Gaskakwattay said "I remember once my grandfather spoke to a boy who had dreams like yours. My grandfather said that God was showing his love to the boy in the dreams. It is a blessing that God speaks to you this way. He keeps you humble. He lets you know that you are insignificant compared to the eternity of his universe. This is how he keeps you on the right path. Every blessing comes with a gift and a challenge. A great blessing we get, is our children. Yet our children are also great challenges. Some blessings come with no gift and only a challenge. I believe that the greatest blessings are also the greatest challenges." She had more to say. "Do not fear death. It is just another step in the journey of our existence. We must all make this journey. To understand the journey, all you have to do is die. Fearing death is like fearing the sunset. It is inevitable. It is not to be feared."

When the week of discussion was over, the vote was finally taken at the elders council. It was nearly unanimous that everyone should have equal access to God. Since God loved them all equally, he would hear their prayers and help them protect the balance that ensured their survival. The Yokuts beliefs would be followed. However, certain Christian beliefs were added, such as repentance and forgiveness. Gaskakwattay was very displeased with this outcome. It was decided to elect a religious leader who would serve a two year term. An elder nearly one hundred years old was elected to be the religious leader. After the election, Estanislao started to realize that he was not happy with the decision to use the Yokuts beliefs. He preferred the Christian beliefs. The Christian God had come to him in a tobacco dream. After much thought, he decided that each person has his own personal relationship with God. Each person should be allowed to believe as he sees fit.

The next day, Gaskakwattay came to Estanislao. "Estanislao, I have come to realize that I love you. In the Chumash way, it is appropriate for me to ask you to be my husband, since I am from the ruling class of Chumash people." Estanislao was surprised to hear this. He said "I do not have rich gifts to give your father, or your family, in exchange for taking you as a wife. This is the custom among Yokuts people when a man marries a rich woman." Gaskakwattay said "My father is dead. My family does not require any gifts from you. They are in Mexico anyway." Estanislao said "I am the son of a messenger. I was not born to marry a Chief's daughter." Gaskakwattay said "My family will be happy for me to marry anyone at this point. There are fewer and fewer men these days." Estanislao said "I would always be beneath your class. I would always be a second class person among your family." Gaskakwattay said "Your victory against the Mexicans has made you a great leader. My family will accept this and will treat you as one of us." Estanislao said "I have not been schooled in the sacred language or the sacred rites. I have no right to learn these things." Gaskakwattay said "Many people become healers and learn the sacred rites who are not children of Chiefs. They do it by not eating meat for one year. Some of them do it by curing others or themselves, even without training. These people are trained at the medical school in Gontop just like the children of Chiefs and Healers. You have done a great thing by defeating the Mexicans. This gives you the right to be trained." Estanislao said "I will pray about these issues and give you an answer as soon as possible."

That evening, Estanislao, Sabulon and three other men entered the sweat lodge. They were preparing to go deer hunting the next day. They sweated and prayed all night long. The next day, before the sun rose, they bathed in the river and rubbed themselves with white sage to hide their human odor. They removed all their human

clothes and wrapped themselves in deer skins with
the fur still attached. The fur still had the smell of
deer. They chewed on white sage leaves to purify
their spirits and give them strength. Estanislao
and Sabulon had deer skins with the heads still
attached. The heads and necks had been stuffed
with tule to make it look like they were still alive.
They walked in the cool morning for nearly two
miles before they found a small meadow with two
deer grazing. Estanislao and Sabulon advanced,
holding their bows and arrows in their left hands.
They crouched over, almost on all fours, to make
themselves look like deer entering the meadow to
graze. The two deer looked up, but were fooled
by the disguises and continued to graze. The
Yokuts belief was that only the pure could approach
a deer close enough to shoot successfully. The
other three men positioned themselves in the
forest to be able to chase a deer after it had been
wounded. Estanislao and Sabulon approached
the deer slowly. When they were within twenty
feet of the deer, they quickly shot their arrows.
They used light arrows made of carrizo cane. The
arrows only penetrated an inch or so and did not
kill the deer. The deer immediately ran toward
the forest. The three men in hiding quickly shot
their arrows at the deer. All five men gave chase
to the deer. Estanislao's arrow had penetrated
the heart of his deer. The deer did not last more
than half a mile. Sabulon's arrow had missed the
heart. His deer ran for a couple of miles before
tiring and succumbing. It had been a successful

hunt. It felt good to carry the deer back to the village. Estanislao and Sabulon did not eat the meat from the deer they had killed. This was the Yokuts custom. Instead, they offered the deer to the elders, who divided the meat among the people.

Nearly two weeks later, Estanislao let Gaskakwattay know that he could not be her husband. It was not the Yokuts way for him to marry above his class. Gaskakwattay was surprised "You are starting a new way of life for your people. Why are you still mired in the past ways of thinking about classes?" Estanislao said "Because with your family, I would always be a second class person."

In the middle of August, 1829, Estanislao was south of the river driving his horses to greener grass. In the distance, he saw someone running. It was hard to see him at first, through the shimmering heat. Eventually he could see that it was a thin, Indian man running well, through the heat. The man ran by at a distance and went toward the river. That evening, Estanislao returned to the village and found Gabriel, who had run in from the Mission Carmel. This was a long distance. Apparently he had run to the Mission Soledad, then San Juan Bautista, Santa Cruz, and San Jose. From the Mission San Jose, he had run east to the Estanislao River. He had taken a wrong turn in the hills and had come out a little too far south. In all, his journey had taken nearly seven days of running. When Estanislao arrived, he was telling his story.

In Spanish he said, "I am Gabriel from the

Mission Carmel. I have come to talk to Estanislao."
One of the Yokuts men asked him, "Why don't you
speak Yokuts with us?" Gabriel said "I am Salinan
and don't speak Yokuts." Estanislao said "Why
have you come seeking Estanislao?" Gabriel said
"He is a man of God. I want to talk to him to ask
him to stop the killing." There was general laughter
at this comment. No one wanted to stop defending
themselves against the Mexicans. Estanislao said
"Who sent you to speak to Estanislao?" Gabriel
said "No one sent me. I came on my own."
Estanislao said "I am Estanislao. I will be glad to
talk with you. Have you eaten yet?"

After dinner, Gabriel and Estanislao
settled down to talk. Estanislao explained that the
purpose of the village was to resist the Mexicans,
prevent them from abducting more children and
teach others how to defend themselves. The
purpose was not to kill. But sometimes killing had
to occur. Gabriel understood very quickly. "I went
to the Mission Carmel in 1780 when I was 30 years
old. I am now 79 years old. I have heard all the
promises made by the Padres. I have seen the
Spanish kill and steal from our people. I have seen
the Mexicans kill and steal from our people. The
Mexicans own all the land now. It is very clear
that no Indian will ever be given land near any
Mission, even after they return the Missions to
us. Yet I stay at the Mission. Do you know why?"
Estanislao said "Perhaps you like the Catholic
religion." Gabriel said "Yes. I am a Catholic. I
can speak to God. He hears me. He forgives me.

He comforts me. There is no better religion that I know." Estanislao understood and agreed. Gabriel went on to explain that the Salinan religion did not give him access to God. He had to speak to God through a religious leader.

Estanislao said "Grandfather, why did you go to the Mission in the first place?" Gabriel said "I lived in a Salinan village with my wife. We lived near the sea. I was a canoe builder. My father was Salinan. My mother was Chumash. I learned to make canoes from my Chumash cousins. One year, the Chief asked me to make a canoe for him so he could fish during the winter and bring food in for the people. I worked hard for nearly six months to make a canoe for him. He paid me with shell money, many strands. During the winter, he went out in the canoe and caught very few fish. His dream of feeding his people went wrong. It was a very hard year. We were all hungry that winter. The Chief had many acorns in his granary. I went to him to buy acorns with my shell money. He said my money was no good. He needed to save his acorns for his own family. I did everything I could to get food for myself and my wife. Everyone in the village was hungry, except the Chief and his family. My wife became weak with hunger. I went to the Chief and begged him to take my money for acorns so I could feed my wife. He said no. I was forced to watch my wife die of starvation. Several other people in the village died of starvation also. I left the village. I was weak with hunger. I walked toward the Mission, which was three days away. I found a few toyon berries to eat. That saved me. I got to the Mission and was fed. I survived. Thank God for saving me."

Estanislao understood. Gabriel's Chief had been a bad man who put his own family before the survival of his people. Among the Yokuts, this would never happen. The Chief was the servant of his people. A Yokuts Chief would have given out all his food fairly so that everyone could share equally. Estanislao enjoyed talking to Gabriel. Gabriel told him stories about the old days, before the Spanish came and about the building of the Missions. Gabriel stayed for three days and spoke with Estanislao every day for several hours. Estanislao was very impressed with Gabriel, who had an unshakable faith.

On the second day, Gabriel said to Estanislao "I am afraid that all you are doing will come to nothing. I have spoken with the Spanish and the Mexicans. In Spain there are many people. Thousands or millions more than we have living in California. In Mexico, there are also many more people than we have in California. If they want to destroy us with a huge army, they can easily do that. They bring their diseases to us, that kill us and prevent us from having children. Our numbers decrease every year. But I have noticed, the ones who survive are the ones who marry Spanish or Mexican people. They are cared for and treated better. I am afraid that one day, most California Indians will be gone. We will be replaced by Mexicans and other people." Estanislao was not surprised to hear Gabriel say this. He had similar thoughts, as did some of the Mexican soldiers Estanislao had spoken to. Yet he would do what he could to protect his people as long as he could.

On the final day, Gabriel said "Perhaps one day Padre Serra, the founder of the Mission system, will be made a saint." Estanislao said "Do you think a California Indian will ever be made a saint? Look at all the suffering our people have been through for the Missions. Yet there are many, like you, who stay with the church. Does anyone ever talk about making an Indian a saint?" Gabriel laughed "No. They just see us as stupid and wild. No Indian will ever be a saint."

Estanislao said "Grandfather, why are you a Catholic?" Gabriel said, "The Christian God comforts me. He is always there for me. He hears my prayers" Estanislao said "Some people think that Jesus was a crazy man, who said he was God so people would give him what he wanted." Gabriel said "Jesus was not crazy. He did many good things for many people. He comforted many people and comforts many people even today. A crazy man does not do good things for other people. Jesus was God. He has blessings for all of us." Estanislao said "The Bible says that Jesus did many miracles. But many people say the things he did were not miracles." Gabriel responded "For believers no miracle is necessary. We know through faith that Jesus is God. For those who choose not to believe, no miracle is enough." Estanislao said "Yet many of the Padres do great evil against us." Gabriel said "Sometimes even very good people, who mean to do the right thing, end up doing great evil. This is because they let fear or greed guide them. They do not trust in God's love."

The next morning, Gabriel took a small sack of chia seeds and ran off toward the west. He was accompanied by three of Estanislao's men, to make sure he found the path back to the Mission San Jose. He would be back in Carmel in five or six days. Of course, Estanislao knew that Gabriel would give a report to the Padres as he returned to Carmel. He would tell the Padres all about Estanislao's village, how many people were in the village and all the military information they wanted.

By late September, 1829, Gaskakwattay was working hard at gathering her things together and bundling up her items and some food. Finally, one day she packed up all her belongings in a large burden basket and without saying goodbye to Estanislao, left the village. This was a very busy time for the village with acorn gathering, salmon fishing and hunting all in progress. Estanislao heard that Gaskakwattay had gone. He was sad she had gone without saying goodbye.

The next morning, as Estanislao was returning to the village from his run, Gaskakwattay appeared before him. She said "Estanislao, I tried to leave but couldn't. I still have unfinished business with you." Estanislao quickly said "You know I cannot be your husband." Gaskakwattay said "Do you remember after the final battle with

Vallejo, I said that you and I had to survive? Do you know why we had to survive?" Estanislao did not know. "I am the keeper of the prayer bundle for my people. Do you know what a prayer bundle is?" Estanislao had heard of them, but had never seen one. "Our prayer bundle is sacred and has been with our people for countless years. I am not supposed to speak of it with you, since you are not of the ruling class. But I feel I should tell you why I must leave. I am the one who protects the prayer bundle and who remembers the stories about each item in the prayer bundle. The prayer bundle is made of elk hide that is wrapped around several items. One item is the fur of a big animal that no longer lives in California. It was called long teeth. It had two teeth that stuck out of its mouth and were longer and thicker than a man's arm. A spear thrower that was used to kill the long teeth animal is in the bundle. There are obsidian knives, spear points, fish hooks and soapstone carvings from famous Chumash Chiefs. Each one with a story about the Chief and what he did for his people. There are other items in the bundle also. This bundle contains the entire history of my people and is our direct connection with God. I must protect it and take it back to my people, so we don't lose our connection with God."

Estanislao understood this and understood that she must take the prayer bundle to Northern Mexico where her brother and his family now lived. She did this to protect the bundle and make sure it continued to stay with her people. She had hidden the bundle in a safe place in the hills to the south. She would retrieve the bundle on her trip to Mexico. She had more to say. "The Chumash people were not the first people in California. When we arrived, there were already people living here. We called them the oak grove people. They hunted the long teeth animals with spear throwers, just like us. But their skin was white. They had long, curly, black hair and beards. One of their spear points, made from chert, is in the prayer bundle. When we first arrived, the oak grove people were many and could easily defend themselves. But we brought colds with us. Colds killed them quickly. Just like the flu kills our people now. After many years there were few of the oak grove people left. We intermarried with them and learned from them. Then there were no more oak grove people, only Chumash. Our elders felt bad that the oak grove people were gone. The elders incorporated some of oak grove people's words into our sacred language. The elders also remembered what the oak grove people had taught about the medicinal plants. We now have a legend that eventually Chumash people will return as white people. This is why we were receptive to the Spanish when they first arrived. We thought they were Chumash returning as white people. But they did not speak Chumash. They did not respect us. They showed us that they were evil and not to be trusted. Most Chumash are very anxious for the Spanish and the Mexicans to leave."

"The Yokuts language does not have a way to say how long the Chumash have been in

California. In Spanish, I would say that Chumash people have been here for about 14,000 years. Your people, the Yokuts, came here about 3,000 years ago. At that time all of California was inhabited by Chumash people. The Yokuts came from the east and brought bows and arrows. The Yokuts lived in villages of 100 people. It was easy for the Yokuts to defeat the Chumash who lived in villages of 20 or 30 people. The Yokuts killed many Chumash in those early years. The Chumash killed many Yokuts, especially after we learned to make and use bows and arrows. Then you learned to intermarry with us and learn from us. Since then, there has been peace between the Yokuts and the Chumash. Then about 2,000 years ago, people came from the west, across the sea, in large ocean going canoes. They traveled with two canoes held together and a sail in between the canoes. They said they were from Tahiti. They looked like us, except darker. They taught us how to make planks from redwood and sew them together to make canoes. We added our asphaltum glue to keep the canoes water tight. The next people who came to visit us were also from the west, across the sea. They called their country Joong Gwa (China). They came in huge ships with many people and animals. They were pale colored, not as pale as Spaniards. They wore clothes made of a soft and shiny material they called see (silk). They wanted to trade with us. But we had nothing they wanted. They gave one of my ancestors a beautiful bright green stone called ju (jade). They stayed only a month or so and never came back. Then, about one hundred twenty years later, Juan Rodriguez Cabrillo came to visit in his ship. He was the first Spaniard. Many Spanish came after that."

Gaskakwattay had more to say "I said, after the fight with Vallejo, that you must survive. The reason you must survive is to be the father of my son. I understand that you do not want to be my husband and come to Mexico with me. But, God has told me, you will father my son."

Estanislao was not attracted to Gaskakwattay. He still thought of her as a man. He told her "I think of you as a man and am not attracted to you." She said "Come with me to the river. We will bathe together, then build a fire to dry ourselves." They spent the day together. Estanislao found that he could easily think of her as a woman. Gaskakwattay ate the leaves of a plant she called sweet tobacco, that Estanislao did not recognize. She said the leaves would make her conceive a son. She also gave the leaves to Estanislao to eat. They smelled like oranges and tasted like pine. The next day, she said "I had a dream last night. I dreamed that one day you will be almost dead, but will be saved by eating yerba santa and mugwort leaves. Remember my dream." After three days of spending many hours together Gaskakwattay said "It is done. I will bear your son in 9 months. I hope you will come to Mexico to visit us. I am grateful to you, Estanislao. Because of you I have finally started to understand something my grandfather told me. God's love is chaos. It is up to you to find what you need in that chaos." Estanislao was confused and said "I don't understand." She said "God's love is chaos. He loves me as much as he loves the Spanish Padres who are killing our people. He loves me as much as he loves the Mexican soldiers who are killing our people. Yet in that chaos, I have found that I love you. In that chaos, we have worked together to produce a pregnancy in me. These are great gifts." She lifted her burden basket and was gone. Estanislao watched her disappear to the west and south.

Estanislao 8. Yoscolo comes

Estanislao found that it was very difficult to be Chief of a village of more than 200. Feeding that many people in the Yokuts way was difficult. The most challenging problem was storing enough food to keep them alive through the winter. Rats, mice and insects invaded stored food. It was easier to rely on their horses to keep them alive. As the number of horses in the village dwindled, Estanislao decided they would have to raid the Missions or the nearby Mexicans and get cattle or horses. After all, they were only taking back what rightfully belonged to the Yokuts people. The Padres had said many times that everything in the Missions belonged to the Mansos. The raids were usually small. They would run into the Mission area at night, take 10 or so horses and run away. This strategy served them well and kept them alive. The Padres were not so angry that they sent out the soldiers after them.

However, the Mexicans were moving closer to Yokuts territory. Governor Echeandia relented to the Padres' requests that there should be a buffer area of settlement to protect the Missions from savage Indian attacks. The Governor gave out large land grants to any Mexican who wanted to live to the east of the Missions. Large herds of cows and horses were given with any land grant. This was very appealing to some Mexicans. They could go from being relatively poor to fairly well off because of a land grant. Of course, the cattle and horses they were given all came from the Mission herds. This all fit in with the Governor's plan to convert the Missions into towns governed by appointed leaders. He had been working on this plan since 1830.

Most of the Mexicans were not interested in working their land themselves. It was much easier to hire other Mexicans or Indians to do the work. Hiring Indians usually meant that the Indians were allowed to live on the rancho, in traditional Yokuts housing. The Indians were fed and given clothing. Sometimes the Indians were paid small amounts in addition to this. The amount they were paid was usually one third what a Mexican was paid.

There were two ranchos in the area that had grown large, with huge herds of cattle and horses. The owners were very mean to the Indians who worked for them. Whipping, raping and even hanging the Indians occurred on these ranchos. Estanislao heard of these events from the Indians who worked on the ranchos. The rancho of Guillermo Castro at San Lorenzo and the rancho of the Peraltas at San Antonio were the worst. Estanislao decided in September of 1830 that it would be good to get the winter food supply for his village from these two ranchos. He lead a force of 80 men to the ranchos. They attacked at night and made off with several hundred head of cattle and nearly one hundred horses. Castro pursued the next morning with seventeen Mexicans in his employ. Estanislao anticipated a pursuit and stayed with thirty men and thirty horses a few miles east of the Castro rancho. The other men headed back to the village with the cattle and remaining horses.

Castro and his men were clumsy in their pursuit. Castro was fat and in no condition to ride a horse for long. Estanislao and his men watched them approach from opposite ridges. The path left by herding all those cows and horses was not hard to follow, even for Castro. Yet the pursuit was slow and took many wrong turns. Estanislao and his men had constructed a corral out of logs and branches to hold the thirty stolen horses. The corral was in the bottom of a valley. Estanislao and his men were on the opposite ridges. The Mexicans fell into the trap easily. They saw the corral and quickly moved to reclaim their horses. Estanislao ordered his men to fire when the Mexicans were within range. The arrows flew at Castro and his men. Estanislao was quick to spot the Romero brothers, who had been part of the Vallejo army. Estanislao had ordered that no one was to be killed. Several were wounded, including both Romero brothers. The Mexicans drew their rifles and returned fire. Estanislao ordered his men into military formation with their bows. He ordered them to lie down. The Mexican bullets flew by without effect. Estanislao and his men continued the fight for three hours. Just enough time to allow the other men, the cattle and the other horses to escape. Then, Estanislao and his men vanished into the oak forest. Castro and his men gathered their wounded and the thirty horses and counted themselves lucky to have survived.

The Hudson's Bay Company came to California in the Spring of 1831. They had been at the rendez-vous in Utah where Jedediah Smith sold his California beaver pelts. They knew that Smith had been kicked out of California by the Mexicans. They also knew the Mexicans were not interested in beaver pelts. So the Hudson's Bay Company petitioned Governor Echeandia to let them trap beaver in the San Joaquin Valley. Echeandia was pleased to allow them to trap beaver. First of all, there was a handsome pay off for him. Second, maybe the trappers could help control the Indians and keep them away from the Missions. He was tired of hearing the whining complaints from the Padres about the latest attack on a Mission. The beaver trappers quickly set up a permanent camp, named French Camp, near the San Joaquin River. The camp was about fifty miles north of the Estanislao River.

William Heath Davis was a wealthy Boston merchant who was curious about California. He sailed his ship the Louisa to California to visit the Mission Santa Clara in the spring of 1831. Davis was fascinated by the Indians. They were so docile in comparison to the stories he had heard as a boy of the ferocious Mohawks and Iroquois. He found that the California Indians were living almost like slaves in the Missions. One of the most interesting Mansos was a tall, strong man named Yoscolo, who was the Alcalde. Yoscolo was 21 and had been born in the village called Laquisimas. Yoscolo was very intelligent, spoke perfect Spanish, could read and write. Yoscolo was one of the only Mansos who could look a white man in the eye. All the others were too shy, or as Davis was to learn, they were afraid that boldness would get them a whipping. Davis was very impressed with the prosperity of the Mission Santa Clara. The fields were large and bountiful. The herds were numerous and well fed. Of course, the Padres hid from him the fact that they were skimming ten or twenty percent of the profit from the Mission by allowing Mexicans to steal from the Mission. The pay off from the Mexicans went into retirement accounts for the Padres.

In May of 1831, a small group of Mansos, lead by Yoscolo, had been put in charge of a herd of cattle. During the night, nearly one quarter of the herd vanished. The Padres decided to punish the Mansos for being stupid and lazy. They did this by ordering Yoscolo to submit to a whipping. Yoscolo knew that the cows had been stolen by Mexicans from Santa Clara who had already paid the Padres under the table for the cows. That night, Yoscolo was locked into the stockade to await his whipping the next morning, in front of the entire Mission. Yoscolo ordered his men to free him. Five hundred Mansos came to his aid. They broke open the Mission stores and took what they wanted. They broke into the convent and freed two hundred female Mansas who were kept there. As they left the Mission, they took nearly two hundred horses. Then they ran into the Mariposa Mountains. Within a few days, Yoscolo and his people found Estanislao. The village called Laquisimas was having a spring celebration. Everyone from near and far had been invited to feast on Mexican cows and horses. There were at least four thousand Yokuts, Chumash and other people in attendance. Most of them had come to respect and thank Estanislao for protecting the people from the Mexicans. It could not be disputed that since Estanislao had defeated Vallejo, fewer children had been abducted for the Missions.

The people welcomed Yoscolo and his people. It was especially good to see that many of the women had not been infected by gonorrhea, perhaps because they had been locked in a convent every night starting at the age of ten. A council of the elders was called to allow Yoscolo to tell his story. Estanislao was not surprised to find, as he listened to Yoscolo, that the story was similar to his own. Echeandia, for all his talk of improvement of the system, had done nothing to help. The Padres continued to steal from the Mansos, with impunity. That night, the elders voted to allow Yoscolo and his people to stay at Laquisimas. However, Yoscolo was charged with the task of helping to feed his people. This would mean more raids on the missions.

The Padres, including Padre Catala, at

the Mission Santa Clara were outraged with the departure of Yoscolo and nearly seven hundred Mansos. This would mean financial ruin for the Mission. They immediately petitioned Governor Echeandia to launch a military campaign and return the Mansos to the Mission. Echeandia was a devout Catholic who could not abide apostates. He ordered the newly promoted General Vallejo to mount an attack. Vallejo had some trouble finding soldiers to help. The Mexican government had not paid them in nearly 2 months. It took three weeks for him to find two hundred soldiers and Mexican volunteers to fight the Indians. Vallejo had to promise to pay some of the soldiers out of his own pocket. Vallejo was especially anxious to prove once and for all that he was better than Estanislao. The American, Davis, went along as an observer.

Vallejo mounted a light cavalry attack, in order to move swiftly against the Indians and take them by surprise. Estanislao received a runner two days later who told him that General Vallejo was on the way with two hundred men. Estanislao was amazed at the arrogance and stupidity of Vallejo. There were nearly two thousand Indians in the area. Some had not gone home after the spring celebration. They wanted to stay and tear the Mexicans to shreds. It would be difficult for Estanislao to protect fat, little Vallejo. He would have to find a way to convince Vallejo to leave without coming near the village. If Vallejo came within a hour's run of the village, a hoard would be unleashed on him that he would not survive.

Estanislao had two days to prepare for Vallejo's surprise arrival.

On the evening of the second day, Vallejo and his valiant two hundred saw some Indians on the bank of the Estanislao River. There were about two hundred Indians by Vallejo's estimate. The Mexicans decided to circle to the south, come back to the north and surprise the Indians on the south bank. The Indians would have no place to go. They would be trapped between the river and the Mexicans. The General also decided to wait until nightfall. Then they would be able to shoot the Indians by the light of their own camp fires. As Vallejo and his army approached the Indians, they were spotted. The Indians immediately took to the water on tule rafts and floated downstream in the swift current. The Mexicans took to the pursuit. It was difficult pursuing the Indians in the dark, through the thick undergrowth along the river bank. After several exhausting hours of pursuit, they finally caught up to the Indians, only to find that the Indians were actually decoy men made of tule and strapped to upright poles on tule rafts. Davis was very amused to see that Vallejo had been out-generalled by Estanislao and Yoscolo. Vallejo returned home empty handed.

The next day, there was a celebration at Laquisimas. The Indians all appreciated the fact that Estanislao had outsmarted the Mexicans using Indian tricks. Not a drop of Indian blood had been shed. The story of the second defeat of Vallejo by Estanislao would be heard throughout California.

Captain John Work of the Hudson's Bay Company set sail from Fort Vancouver, Oregon Territory on the Columbia River in late 1832. He had a party of one hundred men, women and children with him. They were headed to French Camp, near Laquisimas, to establish it as a permanent town. The men were all employees of the Hudson's Bay Company and were beaver trappers. Most of them were French Canadian. They had all started out in Quebec, sailed around South America and had stayed for several weeks in Panama. The storms in Tierra del Fuego had been fierce and had damaged the ship. They got to Fort Vancouver expecting to trap beaver in Oregon. Before they had stayed even a week in Fort Vancouver, the company sent them to California.

As the trip progressed, several of the children and some of the women developed fevers. Within a few days, several of the men had fevers also. The ship doctor recognized the disease as malaria. He treated as many as he could with Jesuit's bark. His supply of the medicine ran out quickly. The ship arrived in the San Francisco Bay and sailed upstream as far as possible. The passengers had to walk the remaining distance to French Camp. The walk would have normally taken about a week. With all the malaria, the walk required more than two weeks. It was a very wet and stormy winter in California. The malaria continued to rage among the trappers and their families. With so many people sick, Captain Work felt he had to return to Fort Vancouver, where medicine would be available. As many as could walk, packed up and returned to the ship for the trip home. They had only been at French Camp for a few weeks. However, the sickest men were left at French Camp, since they could not walk or be carried.

The Spring of 1833 was splendidly green with new growth. Estanislao's horses were well fed from the spring growth. They bred like never before. The mosquitoes were abundant that year. With all the winter rain, there were many breeding pools for mosquitoes. Just a few miles away, in French Camp, there were a few sick trappers, still suffering from malaria. Some of the sick trappers went out trapping beaver, despite their malaria. This quickly spread malaria to the mosquitoes. By April of 1833, many people in Laquisimas had high fevers and violent shaking. Estanislao recognized the disease that had killed Estanislaa immediately. The only thing he could think of was to go to the Mission San Jose and get Jesuit's bark from the Padres. This could cure his people.

Estanislao set out on his run with six other men. They ran for several hours until Estanislao began to realize he was weak from a fever. He sat down on a rock and told the other men to continue on to the Mission and bring back the medicine quickly. After they left, he became weaker and started to shake. He found himself on the ground sweating and shaking out of control. He would have to find some way of spending the night without succumbing to the cold. He crawled to a

large boulder and built a fire nearby. He lay down
between the boulder and the fire to keep warm.
He passed a very cold and painful night. The next
morning, he was so weak he could barely crawl.
He felt that death could come soon. He began
to pray, to the Christian God. As he prayed, he
remembered the words of Gaskakwattay, that yerba
santa and mugwort would save his life. There were
several yerba santa bushes nearby. Mugwort was
growing by the river. He ate as many leaves as he
could and drank some water. He rested all day.
The next day, he felt a little stronger. He ate some
chia seeds and more yerba santa and mugwort
leaves. The next day, two of his men returned to
him from the Mission. They said the Padres had
refused to give them any Jesuit's bark. The Padres
had tied up four of them and had beaten them for
stealing horses. The four were now in jail at the
presidio. The other two had been more cautious
and had not come close enough for the soldiers to
get them. Estanislao asked the two men to gather
as many yerba santa leaves as possible. Then
they helped Estanislao return to Laquisimas.

As the three approached Laquisimas,
they saw many dead bodies lying near the village.
Malaria had already killed over one hundred.
People were dying of malaria at an alarming
rate. Estanislao was shocked to learn that his
brother, Orencio, had been one of the early deaths.
Estanislao was still weak from malaria, but went
around the village teaching as many as he could to
eat yerba santa and mugwort leaves. There were

many people who were already so debilitated, they could not eat the leaves.

Malaria swept through Laquisimas like a sword, killing nearly three quarters of the people. Many were saved by yerba santa and mugwort. A few never contracted the disease. There were so many dead, that the only thing to do was to move the village several miles away. The crows, vultures and condors were allowed to do their work. Several of the survivors turned on Estanislao and blamed him for gathering everyone in a village without a real Yokuts Chief. However, the news had come in from every nearby village that at least three quarters of every village had died from malaria. Estanislao had seen the beaver trappers and had heard that some of them were suffering from malaria. He was quick to teach the people about the beaver trappers, in French Camp, who had brought malaria to California. This made many Yokuts people angry with the Hudson's Bay Company. Some even vowed to annihilate the beaver trappers.

Estanislao recovered from malaria within two weeks and sent out runners in every direction to find the extent of the damage done by malaria. He himself went to several nearby villages. Within a month, the news had come in from all parts of the San Joaquin Valley. The Yokuts people were hardest hit. Several other tribes that lived on the borders of the San Joaquin Valley had also suffered losses from malaria, the Chumash, the Monache, the Miwok, the Tubatulabal, the

Kawaiisu, the Tataviem and the Serrano. After much consideration of the news, the elders decided that probably three quarters of the entire Yokuts population or 20,000 had died from malaria. Malaria would remain a scourge in California for many more years.

The religious leader organized a mourning ceremony for the dead. Everyone was forbidden to eat any meat during the time of mourning. On the first night, two huge fires were built, one for the men, one for the women. They danced slow circle dances around the fires and sang the songs of mourning. The next night, the fires were built again. The songs and dances were sung again. Some of the survivors burned objects or clothing left by the dead. The third night, the two fires were built. Now the songs were sung to encourage the spirits of the dead to fly to heaven. The fourth night, only one fire was made. The men and women came together to celebrate the lives of their lost loved ones. Estanislao mourned the loss of Orencio.

Yoscolo had survived malaria, but was very bitter about the loss of so many Yokuts people from the disease. He blamed all white men for bringing the disease. He blamed the Mexicans for killing Yokuts people. He wanted revenge. He was bold in his speeches at elders' councils. He spoke passionately about doing to the Mexicans and white people what malaria had done to them. There were many Yokuts people who agreed with Yoscolo. He figured that even after losing three quarters of the village, over 250 people still remained. This would be a big enough force to destroy the Mexicans.

Estanislao was very uncomfortable with this kind of talk. After his talk with Gabriel, he had come to realize that the Europeans and Mexicans could easily overwhelm California if they were provoked enough. His talks with Gaskakwattay had taught him that there had been other people in California before the Yokuts. The early people had been wiped out by Chumash or Yokuts people. Perhaps it was the way the world was meant to be. An older people become displaced by newer people. Yoscolo was furious with Estanislao when he expressed these thoughts. Yoscolo became committed to exacting revenge.

Estanislao thought "God has blessings for everyone." How is the loss of 20,000 people a blessing? Has God done this to curse the Yokuts people? Perhaps we brought this on ourselves by opposing the Spanish and Mexicans. He knew this could not be true. Malaria had been brought by Canadians who also opposed the Mexicans. Estanislao slowly remembered something that Gaskakwattay had said "God loves to challenge us." God had certainly given the Yokuts people a great challenge, called malaria.

During the summer of 1833, Yoscolo was elected Chief of Laquisimas. The elders liked to hear him talk about getting revenge on the Mexicans. It was now obvious that the Mexican Army would not attack them anymore. General Vallejo was tired of being humiliated by the Yokuts.

This left the ranchos to fend for themselves. Many of the ranchos were already more like military barracks than cattle ranches, especially those within a days run of Laquisimas.

Yoscolo started to lead the raids for food. Estanislao noticed immediately that sometimes raids occurred even when there was plenty of food. He also noticed that Yoscolo neglected using traditional foods such as salmon, berries, geese, ducks, antelope and rabbits. He seemed intent on eating horses and cows. Yoscolo followed the normal raiding procedure, attack at night, take a few horses and run back to Laquisimas. If the rancho was close enough to Laquisimas, cows might be taken. However, Yoscolo was unkind to any Mexican who chose to pursue him. His favorite procedure was to jump out of the bushes as the Mexicans rode by, knock the Mexicans off their horses, take everything from the Mexicans, including their clothes and whip them until the Mexicans ran back to the rancho.

In August of 1833, a group of American beaver trappers lead by Ewing Young returned to the San Joaquin Valley from the rendez-vous in Utah. Colonel J. J. Warner, a member of the party, observed that the valley was depopulated. In the northern part of the valley, where there had been many Yokuts villages, he saw only eight live Indians remaining. Large numbers of skulls and dead bodies were to be seen under trees, near water and wherever villages had been. He found graves and even what he thought was a large funeral pyre. It was not until the party reached the Kings River that they found a Yokuts village.

There were several American beaver trapping parties in the San Joaquin Valley. Most of them had come in from Colorado and New Mexico, by way of the Colorado River. The Canadians were there also. It only took the trappers a few years to make the beaver extinct in the San Joaquin Valley and in the foothills of the Sierras. The only beavers they left in California were in the San Bernardino and San Gabriel Mountains.

Estanislao noticed that Laquisimas had changed dramatically since the malaria epidemic. Many of the people left in the village had been born at the Mission Santa Clara or the Mission San Jose. They were not fluent in Yokuts and did not know the Yokuts ways. Estanislao and a few surviving elders spent some of their time teaching these people the Yokuts ways and the Yokuts language. Nonetheless, Spanish customs, words and clothing began to be common in Laquisimas. Estanislao was as guilty of using Spanish words as anyone else. He found many Spanish words useful, since there were no similar words in Yokuts.

As the year progressed, Estanislao became very concerned that so few Yokuts had survived. This would be very bad for future generations of Yokuts. He had learned from breeding cows and horses, that a large population is needed to keep the new generation healthy. The more inbreeding that occurred, the worse it was for the next generation. This had been a real problem at the

Mission San Jose one year when too many cows had been slaughtered. Cows were brought in from the Mission Santa Clara to insure that the next generation would be healthy. Estanislao knew that the Yokuts could intermarry with Monache, Paiute and other surviving tribes. But he started to agree with Gabriel that intermarrying with the Spanish and Mexicans would produce stronger offspring. This thought upset him at first. Intermarrying with the Mexicans and Spanish would result in the loss of the Yokuts culture, since Mexicans and Spanish thought of the Yokuts as second class people. However, if intermarrying increased the chances of survival, it would be a good thing.

Estanislao found that he could not practice the Yokuts religion. He had been converted to Christianity the day he had been given tobacco at the Mission and had seen God in a dream. He had become convinced that Christianity was the best way to worship God. The Yokuts religion was a good way to worship God. But Estanislao found more comfort in Christianity. He especially enjoyed the teaching about forgiving one another and loving one another. He could not escape the conclusion that Christianity could make the world a better place for everyone, if Christians were to practice Christianity. After all, God has blessings for everyone.

He expressed these thoughts at elders councils. Yoscolo and others were angry with him for thinking these thoughts. They were stuck on the idea of protecting the Yokuts homeland and keeping the Mexicans out. Estanislao continued to express these thoughts and stopped going on raids. Yoscolo and others became even more angry with him. They accused him of losing his courage. Estanislao grew tired of Yoscolo and his ways. On August 25, 1834, Estanislao and a group of six other Yokuts people from Laquisimas entered the Mission San Jose and asked for forgiveness. Padre Jose Maria de Jesus Gonzales, a subordinate Padre, welcomed them and heard their confessions. At first, the Padre was very afraid. This was the great Estanislao. The Estanislao who had easily defeated the Mexican Army at every battle. Estanislao, now 41, was still a very physically powerful man. He was confident and unafraid. The Padre was surprised to hear Estanislao confess to killing so few Mexicans. He had imagined that much more killing had been committed. The Padre absolved Estanislao of his sins. Estanislao did not feel absolved until the next morning when he ran along the irrigation canal. He ran for nearly two hours and asked God to forgive him. He ran up to the stream where the Ohlone people had lived. Then he turned around and ran back to the Mission. By the end of his run, he felt comforted and absolved. He thanked God for forgiving him and blessing him.

One of the orders of business that Padre Gonzales took care of was the reporting of the deaths of Estanislaa and both of the children. Padre Duran had not recorded these deaths. This was how Padre Duran kept the numbers of Mansos at the Mission higher. Padre Gonzales also recorded the death of Orencio.

Estanislao learned that Padre Rubio had been appointed by the Mexicans to lead the Mission San Jose in 1833. He was the replacement for Padre Duran. His administrator, Jose de Jesus Vallejo, was a very greedy man, and was the brother of General Vallejo. Under Rubio and de Jesus Vallejo, the Mission herds had grown to a reported 35,000 head of cattle. The order for secularization of the Missions came from Mexico in 1833. Secularization meant the Missions were supposed to be divided among the Indians and taken from the Church. Of course, Rubio and de Jesus Vallejo were reluctant to secularize such a financially successful Mission, then valued at $155,000 (a substantial amount of money in those days). The original Spanish promise had been that the Mission would be given to the California Indians who had created it and who had worked it. This did not happen. By 1836, Rubio had convinced Mexico that the Indians in his area were still too wild, rebellious and could not be trusted to run the Mission. The Mission fields, herds, crops and some of the buildings were divided among Mexican settlers in the area, of course to the profit of Rubio and de Jesus Vallejo who received payments from the Mexican settlers. Most of the furniture, tools, books and other valuables ended up on the ranchos of the Vallejo brothers. The Indians became laborers for the Mexicans who now owned the land and herds. The Indians were allowed to live at the Mission or on the Mexican ranchos. Not a single Indian got any land or animals from the secularization of the Mission San Jose. This is how the Spanish promise to the Indians was broken.

Ironically, General Vallejo was involved in creating turmoil of his own. He was part of the Californio movement, a group of liberals who had been born in California to wealthy parents. They were interested in casting off the old ways imposed on them by Mexico. Vallejo thought that California should be ruled by a government with constitutionally limited powers. This lead in 1836 to a revolt lead by his nephew Juan Batista Alvarado. The aim of the revolt, which Vallejo fully supported, was to start their own Californio government, independent of Mexico. Of course, they were not interested in involving the Indians in their plans. The revolt was quickly put down by Mexico. It is amazing that Vallejo and Estanislao both wanted a democratic, or at least constitutional, government in California. Vallejo did not involve Estanislao in his revolt because he thought Estanislao was too stupid and wild. Estanislao did not include Vallejo in his plans because he hated Mexicans.

Yoscolo continued to raid the Mexican ranchos in the San Jose area. He became one of the most hated Indians in California history, hated by the Mexicans and the Padres. A large bounty was placed on his head by the Padres at the Mission Santa Clara. Yoscolo and his men began to wear masks to disguise their faces. He also continued Estanislao's tradition of carving an S with a sword to let the Mexicans know who had been there. In July 1838, Yoscolo and his new ally, Chief Drogo, attacked the rancho of Francisco Perez Pacheco in the Monterey District. The Indians killed Hipolito Mejia and burned down the house of Jose Sanchez. Sanchez rode in pursuit of the Indians and claimed to have wounded seven. A few days later, Yoscolo and his men attacked the rancho of Jose Castro and threatened to kill him if he did not return to Mexico. Then the Indians returned to Pacheco's rancho, ate the corn in his corn field and stayed on the rancho for several days with impunity. The ranchers sent for General Vallejo, who refused to come. This was difficult for the ranchers to accept. Soon thereafter, the body of Eugenio Soto was found hanged and shot full of arrows in the woods near Santa Cruz. Of course, Yoscolo was blamed for this action. Yoscolo was pleased that he and his men were very successful at keeping the Mexicans from invading Indian territory.

Feliciano Soberanes summed up the Mexican frustration in a letter to General Vallejo. "In our area, only a few merchants have one or two firearms" for protection. The rest of us are completely defenseless against the savage Indians. "This is the reason the Indians think they can take advantage of us civilized people." Of course, the letter was completely false. The ranchos were armed like any army presidio, except that most of them did not have cannons.

At the Mission San Jose, the news of

Yoscolo's exploits frightened the soldiers and Padres, and delighted some of the Mansos. Estanislao was glad that Yoscolo was protecting the Yokuts people, but feared that Yoscolo was only delaying the inevitable. He was haunted by something that Gabriel said "Sometimes even very good people, who mean to do the right thing, end up doing great evil. This is because they let fear or greed guide them. They do not trust in God's love."

Estanislao, the great leader of the Yokuts people, who had never been defeated by the Mexicans, lived quietly at the Mission San Jose for the rest of his life. He was regarded as a hero of the Yokuts and other California Indians. Many Indians came to visit him and ask his advice over the years. He continued to advocate peaceful coexistence with the Mexicans. On July 31, 1838 Estanislao died at the Mission San Jose. The cause of death was not reported, but may have been small pox.

Estanislao – Epilogue

Yoscolo's last raid

      Yoscolo continued his raids against Mexican ranchos after Estanislao returned to the Mission San Jose. Yosocolo's hatred of the Mexicans and the Missions was fierce. However, hatred of Yoscolo by Mexicans, Padres and loyal Mansos was also fierce. In 1836, the Mission Santa Clara was secularized, in other words given to the people. The land, buildings and other properties were given to Mexicans. No Indian received anything from the Mission. This made Yoscolo even more angry. In July of 1839, Yoscolo attacked four guards at the Mission Santa Clara. He stripped them naked, left one dead and three wounded. He and his men ran off with several horses. Outraged, Lieutenant Mesa organized a force of soldiers, Mexican settlers and 100 Mansos. Mesa had been soundly defeated by Yoscolo in 1831 when Yoscolo first revolted against the Mission Santa Clara. Mesa took a cannon with him to make sure he could out gun the Indians, who were armed with bows and arrows.

      Mesa moved with amazing speed and was only several hours behind Yoscolo. Mesa pursued Yoscolo into the Santa Cruz Mountains and eventually found him roasting a mare in the pass called La Cuesta de los Gatos. Yoscolo, of course, had prior warning of the approach of Mesa. He had already ordered most of his men to run into the forest for safety. Yoscolo and a few men remained to face the force amassed by Mesa. Yoscolo and his men formed a square and fired their arrows from lying positions. Mesa and his men fired their guns and their cannon. The Mansos shot their arrows. Mesa called several times to Yoscolo to surrender. Each time, Yoscolo's response was "Never, never." The battle continued for some time until Yoscolo and his men had used all their arrows. Several soldiers and Mexicans were wounded in the fighting.

Francisco Palomares, an Indian fighter present at the battle, told the remaining story. Yoscolo was surrounded by soldiers and Mexican settlers, who were only interested in getting Yoscolo. Yoscolo ordered his men to run into the trees, which they did. Yoscolo's brother, Julian, had been injured and walked with difficulty. Then a Yokuts Manso from the Mission Santa Clara called out Yoscolo in his native language. The crowd made a clearing for the two combatants. Each was given a bow and arrow. Starting at 30 paces apart, they took turns shooting arrows at each other, in the traditional Yokuts way. With each arrow, they took a step closer to each other. With each arrow, each man successfully avoided the arrow of the other. Finally, at barely three paces apart, the Manso was able to drive an arrow into Yoscolo's heart. It must be remembered, that the Manso did this to honor Yoscolo, who preferred to die in the Yokuts way with honor, rather than in the Mexican way with no honor.

From the bushes, arrows rained on the soldiers, Mexicans and Mansos. The Mexican settlers were preoccupied with gathering their stolen horses. Several were wounded or died including a Manso named Pedro. In the end, Yoscolo's men ran into the hills to safety.

Anastasio Mendoza, a soldier, cut off Yoscolo's head and tied it by the hair to the pommel of his saddle. He rode back to the Mission Santa Clara with the head prominently displayed. When the soldiers arrived in Santa Clara there were cheers of "Viva" from the Mexican settlers in gratitude for killing Yoscolo and bringing his head back as proof. The soldiers marched triumphantly down the Alameda to the Mission. The Padres at the Mission were so pleased that they allowed the head to be displayed. Yoscolo's head was hung by the hair on a pole for several days in the plaza in front of the Mission.

Estanislao facts and fiction

Estanislao was a real person. Stanislaus County, California and the Stanislaus River are named for him. Modesto is near where Laquisimas was located. This historical novel was written to tell his story in a compelling way. Most of the facts of his life presented in this novel are true, according to historians such Thorne B. Gray as recorded in his book, The Stanislaus Indian Wars. The current novel is an attempt to provide a fictional story that explains why Estanislao may have done what he did. A timeline of the documented facts of Estanislao's life is given below. Most of the characters in the novel were real people. A list of characters is given below, with the fictitious characters indicated. All other characters were real people.

All of the revolts and battles are described as historically accurately as possible. All of the raids against Missions and ranchos are documented in California history and are presented as accurately as possible, except for the first raid at the Mission San Jose, that is completely fictitious. The second battle with Vallejo in 1831 was embellished with the Ghost Dance. However, the Ghost Dance became an important religious movement among California Indians in 1871 and later. The Ghost Dance may have been introduced into California by Nevada Paiute people. This is discussed in Kroeber's Handbook of the Indians of California.

Gaskakwattay is completely fictitious. Gabriel was a real person who died at the age of 142 and is buried in a marked grave in the Mission Carmel. It is not known if Gabriel and Estanislao ever met. The story of Gabriel's life is not known. Te-mi was a real person and an adversary of Estanislao. It is not known if Te-mi aided Vallejo against Estanislao. It is known that Vallejo had Indian allies, other than the Mansos. It is not known how Sucais died. Abraham Laplant was a real person who interacted with Estanislao. The story of his life is not known. All the accounts of Jedediah Smith, his company, the Hudson's Bay Company trappers and other beaver trappers are documented in California history and in Gray's book. It is not known if Smith did anything to help Estanislao. He certainly met with Estanislao many times. William Heath Davis's trip to California is documented in Gray's book.

Life at the Mission San Jose is presented as accurately as possible according to the Sunset book on California Missions, talks with volunteer docents from several Missions and other sources. The raid at the Mission Santa Cruz is documented in the Sunset book. Further facts were learned from docents at the Mission. It is not known with certainty that Estanislao was involved in this raid. If he was not involved, he definitely inspired it. An S was carved into the wall of the Mission Santa Cruz during the raid. It is not known if the Mission Padres actually skimmed from the accounts of the Missions. It is known that the Padres at some Missions did little to stop the open stealing of cattle from the Missions by Mexican settlers. It is also clear that few Indians were actually given Mission land upon secularization. Most Mission land was granted to Mexicans.

Facts about Yokuts culture can be found in Frank Latta's Handbook of Yokuts Indians. Latta's book details the abduction of Yokuts children for the Missions. Facts about Chumash culture can be found in Thomas Blackburn's book, December's Child a book of Chumash oral narratives. The Chumash revolts and Pacomio are discussed in Miller's Chumash, a picture of their world. Facts about California Indian healing can be found in Cecilia Garcia and James Adams, Healing with medicinal plants of the west – cultural and scientific basis for their use.

Characters in the story – All were real people except where indicated

Padres – Narciso Duran, Jose Viader, Buenaventura Fortuni, Diego (fictitious), Pedro Munoz, Jose Maria de Jesus Gonzales, Uria, Antonio Rodriguez, Vicente de Sarria, Ripoll, Fermin Lasuen, Junipero Serra, Catala.

Soldiers – Capitan Alejandro (fictitious), Juan (fictitious), old Pepe (fictitious), Gabriel Moraga, Jose Dolores Pico, Francisco Soto, Ignacio Martinez, Luis Antonio Arguello, Jose Antonio Sanchez, Pina (artilleryman), Lasaro Pina, Juan Bojorques, Andres Mesa, Ignacio Pacheco, Tomas Espinosa, Jose Maria Villa, Nicolas Alvizu, Salvador Espinosa, Mariano Vallejo, Captain Jose De la Guerra, Lieutenant Narciso Fabregat, Sargeant Carlos Carrillo, Captain Pablo de la Portilla, Joaquin Alvarado, Francisco Palomares, Anastasio Mendoza

Governors – Jose Maria de Echeandia, Governor Arguello

Mansos and Indians – Estanislao, Estanislaa, Orencio, Orencia, Estanislao Jr, Sexta, Pedro (fictitious), Rafael (fictitious), Narciso, Pacomio, Maria (fictitious), Chief Te-mi, Diego (fictitious), Cipriano, Cipriana, Ana Maria, Sabulon, Sucais, Yoscolo, Gaskakwattay (fictitious), Matias, Augustina, Chief Drogo, Julian, Pedro

Horse – Noche (fictitious)

Americans – Jedediah Strong Smith, Harrison G. Rogers, Abraham Laplant, men of Smith's beaver trapping group, William Heath Davis, Ewing Young, Colonel J. J. Warner

French – Hyppolite de Bouchard

Mexicans - Guillermo Castro, Peralta, Romero brothers, Francisco Perez Pacheco, Hipolito Mejia, Jose Sanchez, Jose Castro, Eugenio Soto, Feliciano Soberanes

Canadians – John Work, beaver trappers from the Hudson's Bay Company

Time line of documented facts concerning Estanislao

Sept 24, 1821
An Indian man named Cucunuchi, his wife and his mother appeared at the Mission San Jose. The Indian man was renamed, Estanislao (28). His wife was renamed Estanislaa (22). His mother was renamed Orencia (50) and his daughter Sexta (4, d 1823). His brother, Orencio (12), was already at the Mission.

1823
Estanislao became Alcalde, Sexta died in the San Joaquin Valley, Estanislaa gave birth to a son named Estanislao Jr (December) who died before age 2, fall 1825.

February 21, 1824 – revolt of Chumash at Santa Ines, La Purisima (Pacomio was the leader) and Santa Barbara. Pacomio later joined Estanislao. Pacomio, many years later, became the sheriff of Monterey.

1826
Estanislaa and Orencia died at the Mission San Jose of unknown causes.

Jedediah Strong Smith and his trappers visited the Mission San Gabriel. They then proceeded into the San Joaquin Valley.

1827
Estanislao left the Mission San Jose with 400 followers.

1828

Estanislao began night time raids on the mission and ranchos with his followers. They lived, at least partly, on horses.

Estanislao was approached by Indians from the Mission Santa Cruz. A raid was organized to help show resistance and to recruit new help. Raids on other missions and ranchos followed.

Estanislao organized his followers into a 500 man army. Pacomio joined Estanislao. Jedediah Smith's men may have helped Estanislao design his defenses. Estanislao built two forts and tried to recruit other Indians. The Mexicans came after them and were defeated, twice.

Spring 1829
Estanislao prepared for war against Vallejo. The Spanish cannon was too big for his first fort, but was less effective against the second fort. Almost all of Estanislao's men escaped. It is not known how many men were killed by Estanislao.

May 31, 1829
Estanislao returned to the Mission San Jose and begged for forgiveness from Padre Duran. Duran wrote to Governor Echeandia to ask for a pardon for Estanislao.

October 7, 1829
Governor Echeandia wrote a pardon for Estanislao.

1831
Yoscolo and his followers from the Mission Santa Clara joined Estanislao. Yoscolo lead many raids against Missions and ranchos.

Spring 1833

Malaria killed about 20,000 Indians in the San Joaquin Valley area. Most of the Indians were Yokuts. Malaria was introduced by Canadian beaver trappers from the Hudson's Bay Company. Malaria continued in California until it was partially controlled in 1912 by draining Tulare Lake and Buena Vista Lake. This lead to the near extinction of the California condor that depended on the large bird flocks and fish populations at the lakes for food. Malaria was finally eradicated in California after the introduction of DDT.

August 25, 1834
Estanislao returned to the Mission San Jose and died at the Mission July 31, 1838.

July 1839
Yoscolo was killed by soldiers who displayed his head on a pole at the Mission Santa Clara.

The Catholic Church

This story was not written to discredit the Catholic Church. Many California Indians are still Catholics today. The actions of the Catholic Church during Mission times are not condoned in this book. Pope John Paul II addressed the issue of the Catholic Church and American Indians several times. Many American Indians felt the Pope had apologized to them for injustices committed in the past and for taking away their cultural identity. Estanislao was a devout Catholic.

Also by Abedus Press

Healing with medicinal plants of the west – cultural and scientific basis for their use

By: Cecilia Garcia, Chumash Healer
And
James D. Adams, Jr., Associate Professor of Molecular Pharmacology and Toxicology.

Western American plants have been used for thousands of years in healing. This book carefully explains the spirituality of healing and the use of plants in healing. Each of 114 plants has a full color photograph, a description of the plant, its distribution in the American west, traditional uses, active compounds found in the plant and recommendations for use of the plant. Also included are drawings of Chumash pictographs and a brief explanation of their use. The purpose of the book is to teach you how to use these plants in your everyday healthcare.

EASY ORDER FORM
Send form to:
Abedus Press
PO Box 8018
La Crescenta, CA 91224, USA

Please send me _____ copies of Estanislao – Warrior, Man of God. Please send me _____ copies of Healing with medicinal plants of the west. I have enclosed a check payable to Abedus Press.

Cost - $7.99 plus shipping $4.00 = $11.99
California – add sales tax, total = $12.65

Also by Abedus Press
Healing with medicinal plants of the west – cultural and scientific basis for their use.

Cost - $39.95 plus shipping $4.00 = $43.95
California – add sales tax, total = $47.25

Please ship my order to:

Name_____

Address_____

City_____State_____Zip_____

Country_____

Email address_____